HELL'S BELLS
A JUSTICE SECURITY NOVEL
By
T. M. Bilderback

Copyright 2017 by T. M. Bilderback

Author's Note

Hello, reader, and thank you for your interest in this novel.

If you haven't read my first novel, If You Could Read My Mind – A Nicholas Turner Novel, *stop now. Go find a copy. Read it.*

This novel is a sequel to that novel, and there are things in this *novel that you won't recognize if you haven't read* that *novel.*

It was my plan all along to have Nicholas Turner and his "secret weapon" interact with Justice Security. It has taken this long to set the stage for their inclusion.

The Justice Security stories, if you've been a long-time fan, have become darker as the series progressed. One of my personal directives with this series is that no character is safe...no character is immune to being killed, or crippled, or otherwise injured to the point of that character's exit from the series. If the story demands it, that character falls into the darkness.

With this novel, darkness falls. Hard. Brace yourself, and enjoy the ride!

T. M. Bilderback

Chapter 1

"**M**o-om! Madeline's fading my stuff again!"

    "I am *not!* It's just one you haven't found yet!"

"No, it *isn't!* You're lying! You're not supposed to lie!"

"I'm not lying, Karen!"

"You *are!* You're lying, Madeline!"

"*I DON'T LIE!*" The voice came from everywhere at once.

"No fair! You're not allowed to argue with your angel voice! Daddy *said!*"

"Daddy also said not to fade your stuff anymore, and I haven't! So, *hush!*"

"Girls, that is *enough!*"

"But, Mom!" said Karen.

"Meredith!" said Madeline.

Meredith Turner raised her hand, palm out. "Not another word from you two, or I will ground you both! Understood?"

Silence greeted Meredith until she put her hand down.

"Mom?" asked Karen.

Meredith sighed. "Yes, Karen?"

"How do you ground an angel?"

Out of the mouths of babes, thought Meredith to herself. Aloud, she said, "I want you two to finish cleaning this room, then come downstairs. Your father will be home soon, and we have to start dinner."

"Yes, ma'am," said both girls in unison.

Meredith turned and walked out of the room the two girls shared Behind her, she heard Karen say, "I'm sorry, Madeline."

Madeline said, "No biggie, Karen – I just forgot that one."

"Winghead."

"Doo-doo brain."

Meredith smiled as both girls giggled. *They were growing as close as regular sisters...and acting like them, too. Wow...fading Karen's stuff began as a joke. Madeline made Karen's things so that Karen's hand would pass right through whatever she was picking up. It was funny, until Madeline "faded" Karen's bed.* Meredith started down the stairs. At the bottom, in the main foyer of the house, she turned to go to the front door to check on the workers patching the damage to the house. The house had been shot up in a failed attempt to kill her when her daughter, Karen, had been kidnapped by a couple of rogue cops a while ago. After wrangling with the insurance company, Nicholas had asked the local FBI office...well, Marcus Moore...to inquire as to why the insurance company was holding up the claim. The inquiries had their desired effect: the insurance company agreed to repair the house. Replacing the windows was the biggest headache of the whole job.

Had it really only *been* that short a time? *Such a blissful, happy time!*

Meredith had, at an FBI man's suggestion, hired a private detective, Nicholas Turner, to help find Karen. The FBI man was Marcus Moore, best friend to Nicholas. When she had met him, he had been a scruffy-looking ex-cop that had occasional alcoholic binges due to the deaths of his wife and unborn daughter ten years earlier.

Then, the miracle happened that turned *all* of their lives around.

An actual angel had chosen to be reborn into a human baby to re-experience what it was like to live as a human. The baby she had chosen belonged to Nicholas and Janie Turner. After her soul had combined with the sum of the biological contributions of Nicholas and Janie, the baby died, because Janie had developed a fast-forming and devastating uterine cancer. Janie miscarried the baby, and died herself shortly afterward. The baby, a girl who would have been named Madeline Louise, chose to develop as a normal human child alongside her mother in "Heaven". When she was ten, Madeline had exercised her free will to do what few other angels or reborn souls had done before...she chose to come to Earth to assist her father with getting his life back on track. Madeline had a few surprises in store for her father, however.

Madeline could be what Nicholas, Meredith, and Karen called "faded". That meant that she was see-through, and worldly objects passed through her. She could also make herself solid if she chose. However, if she chose to be solid, she was also vulnerable, and could be hurt or killed like any normal human. Madeline could make worldly objects faded as well, by touching them when she was solid, then fade again along with the object. She could be invisible when she chose. She could also fade other people, and transport them with the speed of thought. She could take people to higher realms of existence, and she could shoot bolts of pure white power from her hands. These power bolts were harmless to those creatures of good heart, but could immobilize, or even kill, those that embraced evil.

Madeline could also communicate with her father telepathically.

Either father.

Because, even though Madeline had chosen to live out a life as a human child with angelic powers, she was still half angel, and answered to a different father as well as to Nicholas. But, since Madeline had free will, she could stay with her earthly father as long as she wished...and she would continue aging as if she were a normal little girl.

Meredith still sometimes found it hard to believe. When something happens in your life that literally confirms that the afterlife exists, that angels exist, that souls exist, that *God* exists...well, it can be overwhelming.

Overwhelmed or not, Meredith was now the stepmother of an angel.

And she *loved* it!

Meredith opened the front door just as one of the workers outside threw down a ruined upstairs shutter from the top of a ladder. When it hit the ground, it exploded like a gunshot, causing Meredith to scream and jump.

Almost instantly, Madeline faded in beside her, in full "angel", or "battle" mode. Her body glowed with white non-light, and her eyes were a bright, penetrating deep blue. Sparks came from her hands, and her power cascaded from each shoulder in a fall that resembled wings. Her eyes searched for the threat that had made Meredith scream.

Meredith had only seen Madeline in "battle" mode one other time, and that was when the little girl had helped take down George Parker, the dirty cop behind Karen's kidnapping. The sight was both comforting and frightening...and not for other human eyes!

"Madeline!" hissed Meredith "It was nothing! Back out of the doorway before someone sees you, honey!"

Madeline turned to Meredith, focusing those glowing blue eyes on her. Seeing the truth there, Madeline backed into the house, gradually becoming her normal self.

"I'm sorry, Meredith," she whispered "I thought something was wrong."

Meredith smiled and hugged Madeline close. "Oh, honey, everything is fine. You did nothing wrong, my sweet darling! Thank you for watching over me!"

"Everything okay, Mrs. Turner?" said a voice from the doorway.

Both Meredith and Madeline jumped at the sound. The job foreman stood in the doorway.

"I heard you scream...did the shutter scare you?" he asked sheepishly. "I'm sorry...we'll try to be more careful."

"No, that is fine," replied Meredith. "I was daydreaming, and the sound startled me."

"We should be finished by tomorrow evening," said the foreman. "Then we'll be out of your hair."

"Thank you," said Meredith.

The foreman smiled at Madeline. "I promise that the house will be as good as new, little Miss."

Madeline returned the smile. "Thank you, sir."

The foreman mock-saluted as Meredith closed the front door. Meredith, pressing her back against the door, looked at Madeline, who was looking up at Meredith. Suddenly, both started giggling and laughing.

Karen, having heard the laughter, started down the stairs. "What's so funny? Wha'd I miss?"

Of course, neither could explain to Karen what was funny, which made them both laugh harder. Karen crossed her arms and frowned, but she shortly joined into the contagious laughter. Soon, all three were flopping on the foyer carpet, tickling each other. Finally, spent, they sprawled side by side, with Meredith in between the two girls, all of them trying to catch their breath.

"Meredith?"

"Yes, Madeline?"

"Thank you."

"For what?"

"For not calling you a winghead?" asked Karen.

"No, poophead," answered Madeline. "For loving me. And for liking me."

Meredith, puzzled, said, "Why would I not love you, or like you, Madeline?"

Madeline was quiet for a moment, then she said, "Because I was Daddy's daughter. From before. And because I'm an an...anom..."

"Anomaly?"

"Yeah," she replied. "I'm really not supposed to be here, Meredith...not the way I am."

Karen propped herself up on one arm, facing Meredith so that she could hear Madeline better. "What do you mean the way you are?" she asked.

Madeline smiled. "Angels...or what humans *call* angels...have been reborn before. Most times, their memories have been wiped clean, and their powers were sup...sup..."

"Suppressed?" supplied Meredith.

Madeline nodded "Yeah. Or, they used their free will to give up being an angel to fall to earth so they could live normal lives as humans."

"So why are you an an...anom...anemonae?" asked Karen.

Meredith smiled. "Anomaly, Karen."

Madeline turned on *her* side, facing Meredith. "Because I used *my* free will to come to earth and live...but I also kept my powers." She smiled. "With Mom's blessing...and His."

Meredith said, "I like you just fine, sweet Madeline. And I love you, as if you were my own daughter. I did not know that it was with God's blessing, Madeline. Why did he give you his blessing?"

Madeline flopped back down onto her back. "In the realm that humans call 'Heaven', I'm one of His most powerful warriors," she said matter-of-factly. "Only Michael, and the other archangels, and maybe a couple of other regular angels, are more powerful. But, there are *two* realms...and the other is dark, painful, and evil. Humans call it 'Hell', and it's where souls go that are bad. They have warriors, too...some as strong as Michael. The leader there is His enemy, and is almost as powerful. 'God', as you call him, sent me here because something big is coming, and I don't know what it is, and I don't know when, and Daddy's going to be right in the middle of it." A silent tear ran from her eye. "I was told he'd need all the help he can get...and he *still* may not win. And I may not win. But it isn't here yet." She moved her head so that it rested on Meredith's arm. "Doesn't stop me from worrying, though..."

"STOP!" SHOUTED NICHOLAS Turner. "Don't move!"

"Well, you know, I hadn't planned on it, Nicky," said Snickers, computer programmer, snitch, and former junkie. "When ya asked, you know, for me to come give you a hand, you didn't tell me that, you know, it was gonna be to hang pictures on your walls."

Nicholas chuckled while he marked the picture's location so that he could drive a nail. "You would have come anyway, Snick...you don't fool me a bit."

"You know, Nicky? You know me too well."

"Okay, buddy, you can put it down now."

Snickers sighed as he put the framed print down and leaned it against the wall. "You been doin', you know, pretty good since you busted, you know, that Parker cop, haven't you?"

Nicholas nodded. "Yeah, business *has* picked up quite a bit." He shrugged his shoulders. "I think I've missed some because I've been out of the office so much lately. My paperwork has backed up like crazy because I don't have time to do it the way I should. It's hard to do it all alone."

"Can your, you know, new wife help out with any of it?"

"I wish she could, but her artist commissions have doubled since the Parker bust, too. The whole story with Karen's kidnapping, my busting the case open with *your* help, our jobs, and our marriage all came together enough to really turn things around for both of us." *Not to mention Madeline's help...I wonder how much of this is because of her?*

Snickers handed Nicholas a nail and the hammer. "Maybe you need, you know, one of those secretaries or something, you know?"

Nicholas hammered the nail into position. "I've thought about it I can afford one now...maybe to come in part-time, a few days a week...". He hung the picture on the nail, straightened it, then backed up a step to admire it. "I'm just not sure that I can find someone dependable enough to do the job, but is flexible enough to do the job part-time. Someone that won't freak out if I bring in a banged-up kid, or have to shoot some poor schmuck that objects to paying child support and goes rowdy on me."

"Speakin' of, you know, work," said Snickers, "Whaddaya, you know, got goin' right now?"

Nicholas smiled. "Believe it or not, old buddy, I just finished one up, and I don't have another one on the horizon. For now, anyway. Why?"

Snickers shrugged. "I ain't, you know, sure yet. Give me, you know, a couple of days, and I might, you know, be able to drive some business, you know, your way."

Nicholas was touched. Snickers was one of his best and most reliable stoolies. He had known Snickers since his early cop years. As a street patrolman, Nicholas had arrested Snickers for robbing a liquor store. Snickers immediately began offering information about anything Nicholas wanted to know, as long as Nicholas didn't lock him up. Nicholas made a counter offer: if the information turned out to be accurate, he would make the charges go away.

The information was accurate, and Nicholas was true to his word. Their give and take relationship grew, and information from Snickers was directly responsible for Nicholas's promotion to Detective. As a gift, Nicholas paid for Snickers to enter a good rehab clinic to clean himself up.

A grateful Snickers still kept in touch with his underground connections, but he remained clean. He had a knack for computers, and held a job as a computer programmer. He was a small, ratty-looking man, and still had the nervous twitches that he had developed as a junkie. He hung out most nights at McFeely's, a bar in the Hollow. McFeely's, commonly known on the street as "McFeelme's", was a tough place that served hard drinks to harder customers, and had a reputation of being able to provide almost anything that a person might be looking for.

Madeline had told him that Snickers adored him, and looked at him as a big brother. And she wanted to meet Snickers. Since Madeline was what she was, that spoke volumes to him about Snickers.

"Well, I always appreciate more business," replied Nicholas. "I don't suppose you can give me an idea yet?"

"Nah...you know, I have to convince, you know, this guy that you're, you know, legit."

"*Legit?*"

Snickers chuckled. "Nicky, you know what I mean! I have to make sure he believes that you won't, you know, turn him in...or treat him like, you know, crap just because he's an ex-con, you know?"

Nicholas smiled at his friend. "I gotcha, Snick."

"I mean, you know, that just because you're, you know, a detective, I gotta convince him that you're not, you know, that *kind* of detective."

"That *'kind'* of detective?"

"You know, Nicky! I mean, like you're, you know, a *private* dick!"

"Well, I do my best to keep my dick private. Meredith says I do, anyway."

Snickers smirked. "Ha, ha, funny. I dunno, you know, about the private part, but, you know, you *are* a dick!"

Both men lost control because of the juvenile humor, and began laughing uproariously.

LATER, AFTER THEY HAD finished hanging pictures, they locked the office door and moved to the back room, which had previously been the living quarters for the private detective.

"So, uh...how's your, you know, new marriage? Everything, you know, goin' good, Nicky?" asked Snickers.

Nicholas nodded. "It's great, Snick. You should find some nice girl yourself...nothing beats coming home to people that love you."

Snickers shook his head gently while smiling an odd smile. "I don't, uh, you know, don't think so, Nicky, you know? No girl's gonna, you know, look at me and say, you know, *that's* who I want to, you know, spend my life with. It just don't, you know, happen that way."

A knock came on the outer office door. The two men looked at each other, surprised. It was 5:30 PM, and, officially, the office was closed.

Nicholas made a face. "Ahh, why not? Might be a client, Snickers."

"Mind if I, you know, disappear out the, you know, rear entrance?" asked Snickers. "Gonna head, you know, down to McFeelme's."

"Sure, buddy, I'll catch you later. Stay out of trouble."

Snickers ducked out the rear entrance as a knock sounded on the office door again.

"Coming!" called Nicholas.

Nicholas crossed to the door and unlocked it. When he opened it, a woman was standing there.

The woman appeared to be in her mid-forties, mouse-brown hair with gray streaks, shoulder length. Nice figure, settled firmly in middle age. About five-one, wearing a nice pastel blue dress to just below her knees, with an understated pearl necklace and pearl earrings.

"May I help you?" asked Nicholas.

The woman smiled. "Hello, Mr. Turner." She held out her hand, and Nicholas shook it. She had a firm grip, but not overpowering. "My name is Cindi Moore. I was hoping to speak to you about some part-time secretarial and bookkeeping work."

Nicholas was stunned. The only person he had mentioned the idea of a part-time person to was Snickers, and that was just a few minutes ago. So, unless Madeline had been inside his head again, this particular idea had been answered from a much higher source. Or it was a huge coincidence.

Nicholas smiled at the woman. "Please come in, Ms. Moore."

Cindi returned the smile. "Thank you, Mr. Turner." She stepped into the office.

Nicholas closed the door and gestured to his desk. "Please sit down."

Cindi sat in the client chair. Nicholas settled in behind the desk.

"Well, Ms. Moore, what brings you to me?"

Cindi smiled. *Nice smile*, thought Nicholas. "It's a very short story, Mr. Turner. I seem to find I need a job, after I sort of...*fell* into the city."

"That sounds intriguing, but, why me?"

"I've been hearing about you a lot lately, Mr. Turner, through the newspapers and television. I felt that your business might be expanding enough to justify hiring someone to keep your office for you, so I came to see you. I love children, and I realize that it's not always fun doing what you do. I have secretarial skills, I can write reports, I have bookkeeping skills, and I can keep my head in an emergency, and part-time hours would be perfect for me right now."

Hi, Daddy! said Madeline inside his head.

Hi, sweetpea!

Meredith says that dinner is almost ready.

I'll be along shortly, sweetie.

I'll tell her. I love you!

I love you, too!

"Mr. Turner?"

Nicholas shook his head and smiled. "Sorry, Ms. Moore. Woolgathering."

Cindi smiled. "I understand."

"How about Mondays, Thursdays, and Fridays?" Nicholas named the hours, and a generous pay rate.

"That's fine, Mr. Turner. I accept the job."

"Great! But you have to call me Nicholas, and I'll have to do a background check on you."

"Only if you call me Cindi, and I'll bring all the paperwork you need for your background check. When would you like to start?"

"Would tomorrow be okay with you?"

Cindi smiled again. "It would."

They both stood, and Nicholas shook Cindi's hand. "Welcome aboard, Cindi."

"Glad to be employed, Nicholas. I'll be back first thing in the morning."

SNICKERS HAD HUNG AROUND the back entrance long enough to peek through and see who was visiting Nicholas. When he saw Cindi, something 'dinged' inside his head, and he decided to hang around outside the building that housed his detective friend's office.

If someone had asked Snickers why he wanted to follow this woman, he would not have been able to offer a cohesive answer. Something inside him just told him to find out more about her, that Nicky needed to know, and Snickers listened to his hunches.

He was across the street from Nicholas's office, inside the small convenience store, watching the entrance to the building. After about fifteen minutes, Cindi came out of the building, stopped for a moment, and seemed to be looking at nothing.

Snickers felt a shiver down his spine, but he knew she couldn't see him. He was back a few feet inside the store, watching through the store's big windows in the front, and it was a bright, sunny late afternoon. *No way* could she see him. *Jitters, I guess*, he thought to himself.

Cindi smiled to herself, turned left, and began walking toward downtown. Snickers, on the opposite side of the street, left the store and began walking in the same direction. He was about half a block behind her. *Maybe she's going to McFeely's!*

Snickers had been following Cindi for a couple of blocks when she suddenly crossed the street diagonally, still heading downtown. Snickers slowed his pace a bit, and that put her about half a block in front of him, but on the same side of the street. He slowed down a little more, giving Cindi just a little more space between them, lessening his chances of being spotted. Suddenly, Cindi turned the corner.

Snickers sped up a bit, because he didn't want to lose her. He turned the same corner that Cindi turned just seconds ago.

The woman was nowhere in sight.

Snickers stopped in his tracks. Along the street ahead of him, he saw about five people, and none of them were Cindi.

Okay, wot ta fuck's goin' on here? Where she go?

Snickers walked up to the alley between the corner building and the next. It was dark, and full of shadows. He did not see Cindi there.

He whirled back around and started looking along the street again. *Now I'm havin' a bad feelin' about this...*

Snickers had barely finished the thought when a pair of hands grabbed his shoulders and pulled him off of his feet into the shadows of the alley.

"Let's you and I have a long talk right now," said Cindi, from the dark.

Chapter 2

Justice Security, Incorporated owned its own building on a tree-lined street in a better part of the city. The six-story aboveground edifice occupied a large portion of a city block, with parking areas for visitors, and a landscaped, park-like green area on its south side. The building itself was constructed of three-foot-wide reinforced concrete walls. Each window was made of thick bulletproof glass, including the visitors' entrance door. The building extended six floors underground. The bottom three underground floors were used as a vehicle storage area, and housed various armor-plated and bullet resistant vehicles to be used as protective equipment for transporting and defending employees or clients. The next underground level was the armory. All types of weapons were stored in the climate-controlled armory, from revolvers and automatic pistols, to mortars, to surface-to-air missiles and launchers, and various armor-piercing weapons. Enough weaponry and ammunition were stored in the armory to take down a small country's government, should they be hired for such a thing...and they had done so, twice, a couple of years ago under an ultra-classified government contract. The floor above the armory was records storage. This floor contained the paper files, computers, data storage, and research areas needed for executing and completing client contracts. The final underground level was the garage for employee parking, and was accessed by a ground-level entrance contained by a thick, heavy steel door embedded into the concrete walls of the building.

At ground level, the first floor contained the reception area, the cafeteria, building security, the medical facility, and visitors' lounge. The second and third floors were occupied by employee offices, conference rooms, smaller meeting rooms, and clerical services. The fourth floor housed executive offices and the situation room. The fifth floor was for guest housing, and the top floor contained residential apartments for the top level people of the company. The roof of the building had a helicopter pad, equipped with two armor-reinforced, stealth-equipped, black ops helicopters always ready to fly at a moment's notice.

The company also owned a private jet and two large cargo planes, which were housed at a private airfield just south of the city. Once, there was a second jet, but it had been shot down earlier over the Mojave Desert in Nevada.

Justice Security had been formed a few years earlier by four college friends, who remained the directors. They had added two more partners, and, more recently, one more when Justice Security's main competitor, Jim Dandy, joined them. The seven partners were the owners and sole stockholders of the company.

Joey Justice, after whom the company was named, was a nondescript man. Standing at five feet ten inches, he had dark hair and intense brown eyes that usually missed nothing. He had founded the company with the premise of providing security services tempered with justice, as his name implied. He was very much in love with the lady in his life, who was also one of the co-founders of the company.

Misty Wilhite, the lady of Joey's life, stood five feet five. She had shoulder-length auburn hair, with green eyes. She was extremely attractive, but she had a punch that could drop a person twice her size. She, too, was very much in love with Joey, and shared his belief of security and justice. They had not married yet, but had just become engaged.

Dexter Beck was the resident computer nerd. Standing one inch taller than Misty, Dexter was consistently underestimated by antagonists. Understanding usually followed, because Dexter also was a martial arts master, utilizing several methods of self-defense. The security and computer systems used by Justice Security were created, programmed, and maintained by Dexter.

Percival "King Louie" Washington was the fourth founding member of Justice Security. Louie stood four inches over six feet, and had a very imposing muscular build. He also was very intelligent and street-smart. His skin was the color of a chocolate bar, and he kept his head shaved. The other three founding members had nicknamed him "King Louie" in their first year of college because of his unfortunate facial resemblance to the cartoon character in the Jungle Book movie. It wasn't racial, and Louie knew it...just like if he had had a big nose, they would have nicknamed him "Baloo". Besides, anything was better than his given name of Percy.

Recent additions to the partners included Jessica Queen, the former executive secretary to the four partners. Her immediate replacement, Patti

Hoehn, had been tortured, killed and mutilated by Esteban Fernandez, who had caught her on the street snapping photos during the first encounter of him by the company. Patti's replacement, Turk Wendell, was a huge, hulking man, who was surprisingly adept at performing secretarial duties.

Another addition to the partners had been Dexter Beck's right hand person, Megan Fisk. She had led an attempted pre-emptive attack on Fernandez, and had gotten wounded in the process. She and Dexter had eloped, and were happily married newlyweds.

Jim Dandy, a former competitor of Justice Security, was the seventh partner. Standing two inches over six feet, Jim resembled a young Tom Selleck.

Each weekday morning at nine, the partners met in the situation room to discuss current and recurrent cases. If, for some reason, they couldn't be there in person, they would link into the meeting by a secure satellite feed. This was a requirement of the partners, because it kept everyone in the company informed of the status of the cases handled by each of the partners, should someone else have to step in to complete a case, or should a bailout or rescue become necessary. Since their cases had taken them all over the world, into some fairly dangerous situations, bailouts and rescues sometimes were a necessity.

That morning, the same morning that Nicholas Turner's new secretary was scheduled to begin work, the regular nine o'clock morning meeting at Justice Security was being held at eight o'clock, in the situation room. The reason was an important development in a case in London, and the time difference dictated that the meeting be held earlier.

Jim Dandy was overseeing construction of a second Justice Security location...it was a hiding place, should it ever become necessary.

Once the London update was out of the way, the partners turned their attentions to more pressing matters.

"What I want to know is this," said Louie. "We took the fight to Fernandez in Chicago, so what do we do next?"

"Good question," said Joey "I guess we all need to talk about this and work out a plan of action."

"After what happened to Louie with his girlfriend, and with Joey at that night club, I guess we're all just a little paranoid," said Dexter. "I mean, how do we trust clients now? Or people that we meet in our personal lives?"

Megan stifled a yawn. "Ohhh, sorry. Somebody kept me up late last night," she said, with a significant glance at Dexter. He blushed. "We also need to be rebuilding our ranks. Donna really decimated our grunts that night, and so did Fernandez in Chicago."

Jessica said, "That's in progress. We've hired several people. They're in training now. And we have Jim's people, too."

Jim smiled. "My people are very good, and can hold their own wherever they're placed."

"The people that were killed by Donna were trainees and service people, like cafeteria workers and janitors," added Misty. "We weren't expecting an attack from 'within our own ranks', so to speak."

"Donna's connection to Fernandez was so deep, I don't think we could have found it without digging deep enough to be obvious to everyone," said Louie. "And who's going to suspect a popular fashion model, anyway?" He shook his head. "Man, I wish those nightmares would stop! I can't get no sleep, and it's makin' me really grouchy!"

Everyone nodded their agreement.

Joey said, "Well, turning back to the war with Fernandez..."

He was interrupted by the entrance of Turk Wendall. Turk looked disturbed.

To Joey, Turk said, "Phone call, boss. You better take this one. On speaker. Recorders are going."

For Turk, that meant it was life or death, because Turk didn't say "shit" if he had a mouthful, and he had just said several sentences, and had started the recording equipment.

None of the partners said a word in reply. Joey reached out to the telephone, and pressed "speaker". The call came through discreet speakers unobtrusively placed around the room.

"This is Joey Justice. May I help you?"

"Hello, Joey Justice," replied a man with a deep Southern drawl. "Mah name is Gary McGee."

"What can I do for you, Mr. McGee?"

"Well, for starters, you can follow instructions to be at a certain place and let mah people pick you up and bring you to me."

"I see. And why would you want me brought to you?"

"Well, that's easy," replied McGee "That way, I can peacefully take you to the man with the money."

Joey chuckled. "And that man is...?"

"Esteban Fernandez."

Joey's eyes widened in disbelief. He then looked around the table at his friends.

"Mr. McGee, I'm afraid I will have to decline your kind offer. When I meet with Fernandez again, it will be at a place and time of my own choosing."

"That's unfortunate, Mr. Justice."

"And why is that, sir?"

The voice sounded saddened. "Because all thirty-seven of those poor children will die."

"What children, McGee?"

"Turn on the news, Mr. Justice. It's all over the TV." Then came the sound of a disconnected phone line.

Misty had already turned on the monitors in the situation room, and tuned them to Channel 7 in the city.

"...and we don't know where the children, or the bus driver, are at this moment," said Miriam Apple, a reporter known as a friend to Justice Security. "Repeating, a school bus loaded with thirty-seven children, and their bus driver, have been kidnapped. Several witnesses stated that four people, faces covered with ski masks, and carrying automatic weapons, stormed the bus, and loaded the children and the driver into two black vans. The vans were driven away, but police have not...wait just a moment...". Miriam pressed her hand to the earpiece in her ear. She looked again at the camera. "I'm told that we have one of the kidnappers on the phone with us right now. Caller, can you hear me?"

The voice that answered Miriam was the same voice that the partners had just heard on their own phone. "Yes, ma'am, ah sure can."

"Sir, can you tell us if these children are safe?"

"Well, they are for right now."

"And the bus driver?"

"She's with the children, of course."

"You said that they are safe 'for right now'. Does that mean that they might be in danger?"

A sigh was heard from the telephone at Channel 7. "Let me explain to you what's happenin', darlin'. We took that busload of children...and their driver, of course...and have put them somewhere safe, but away from everyone. The location is known only to me and my...co-workers, shall we say. However, we have installed some...insurance...to make certain that we, and only we, can open up the safe place that we have put them. If someone stumbles onto their hiding place and tries to open it up without knowin' *how* to open it, several hundred pounds of C-4 explosive will go off, killing everyone within a city block of the place."

Miriam's eyes had widened on screen as she listened. "That's horrible!"

McGee chuckled "That's not all, ma'am. If we...or those we have instructed as to how to open the place...don't disconnect the explosives properly by five o'clock this afternoon, the timer will trigger the explosives. Unless we get what we want, of course."

Joey spoke quickly. "Turk, get Marcus Moore on the phone. Tell him to get here as fast as he can." The company often contracted with the United States Government, and Marcus Moore was the city's FBI Section Chief, and their liaison. They currently had an official contract to pursue Esteban Fernandez as an enemy of the United States of America...that was why they were discussing ways to bring the fight to the drug lord.

"Yeah, boss." He went to the phone at his desk to call.

"What exactly do you want, sir?" asked Miriam.

"I want Joey Justice. There's quite a price on his head offered by a certain individual, and I want that bounty. I aim to turn him over to Esteban Fernandez, and I aim to collect that bounty from him."

"Holy *shit!*" shouted Louie. "Another damn *wannabe!* I knew those assholes in the park wouldn't be the last ones! Don't this damn farce *ever* stop?" He pounded the conference table with his fist as he exploded.

Misty patted Louie's arm. "*Easy,* big guy...nobody has Joey yet."

Louie looked at her with a storm on his brow. "Emphasis on the 'yet', little girl. I'm scared that it's just gonna be a matter of time."

Turk came into the situation room. "Marcus on the way, boss."

Joey nodded "Thanks, buddy. You might want to stay here for a few minutes, Turk...and is Tony here yet?"

Turk nodded.

"Call him. He needs to be in here, too." To everyone else, he said tiredly, "Shit. I hope nobody had anything else to do today."

On the monitors, Miriam Apple had continued questioning McGee.

"Sir, would you be willing to tell us your name?" asked Miriam.

"Girl, I think you're tryin' to hoodoo me, but I don't see any harm in telling you. My name is Gary McGee. I have already telephoned Joey Justice, and explained the situation to him."

"Can you tell us Mr. Justice's response, Mr. McGee?"

"Hmmm...what was that line from that pirate movie? I can't remember...but, Mr. Justice chose to refuse my invitation. I told him that was unfortunate, and that he should turn on the teevee. Then, I hung up."

"Would you consider disclosing to me the location of the children?"

The phone disconnected. Miriam held her earpiece to her ear, then began going over the salient details of the kidnapping for new viewers.

TONY ARMSTRONG, THE uniformed grunt in charge of the rest of Justice Security's grunts, and keeper of the front desk, entered the situation room.

Joey and the others quickly brought him up to speed on the current crisis, then Joey gave him instructions.

"Use the encrypted channel on our new radios, and get in touch with as many grunts as you can. Turk and the rest of us will begin with the plainclothes personnel. We need every piece of information we can get on these kidnappers, and we need it by noon. Who they are, where they are, how are they armed...we gotta know, and we gotta know *now*. Everyone is to use money, threats, and pain to get the answers. Understand?"

Tony smiled. "You got it, Joey." Tony left for the front desk.

"Turk?"

"On my way, boss." He left for his desk down the hall.

Two minutes later, the phone in the situation room buzzed. Joey answered. "Yes, Turk?"

"Marcus Moore on line one, boss."

"Thanks," said Joey. He pressed line one on the speaker phone.

Traffic noises could be heard in the background.

"Hello, Marcus," said Joey. "You're on speaker phone, and all of the partners are here now listening. Are you fully aware of the situation?"

"Yeah, and listen, Joey, I have a suggestion," said Marcus. "No, actually, it's an order, as your liaison, and as the Section Chief in charge of the kidnapping. I was going to wait until I got there, but I'm stuck in traffic on the damn interstate."

He continued, "We need a kid specialist on this one, Joey. I want you to call Nicholas Turner, and get him over there. I would call him, but I've got to call the Bureau, and get them ready for some broken procedures. Offer him a thousand a day, with a big bonus. The Bureau is good for it."

Joey looked at his partners. "Marcus, are you sure?"

"This one's too big to handle alone, buddy-boy. We need somebody that specializes in children's cases, and that's Nicky...on this one, there really isn't anyone else, because he has a special...talent, we'll say, for locating missing children. So, get him over there, wouldja please?"

Chapter 3

Nicholas arrived at his office at eight forty-five that morning. Cindi was already waiting for him in the hallway.

"Good morning, Mr. Turner," she said to Nicholas.

"Oh! That's right! Good morning, Cindi!" he replied.

"Isn't it a beautiful morning, sir?"

Nicholas smiled as he unlocked the door. "Yes, it is...and aren't you supposed to call me Nicholas?"

Cindi smiled demurely. "Yes, sir."

Nicholas opened the door, and let Cindi enter first. He followed, and closed the door behind him. He looked around the office. He actually did have two desks, but one was covered with a computer, a phone, and assorted clutter...and was the desk at which he normally performed his work. The other desk also had a computer and a phone...and a large stack of paintings Meredith had painted and given to him to decorate his office a bit. This desk also was closest to the file cabinets. He gestured to it.

"I guess you can use that desk, if that's okay with you," he said to Cindi.

"That will be great, sir," she replied.

Cindi walked over to her desk, took her purse from her shoulder, and tucked it into one of the desk drawers. She checked the rest of the drawers, and pulled out pens, pencils, memo pads, legal pads, and other materials that she might need.

"Now, then, that's better," she said. "Ready for anything. Where would you like me to start?"

Sheepishly, Nicholas said, "Would you mind hanging those paintings for me?"

Cindi smiled "I'd be delighted!"

"Thank you. That would save me all kinds of time."

As Nicholas sat down at his work desk and began checking his computer, Cindi began looking through the paintings.

"Did your wife paint these?"

"Hmm? Oh...yes, she did."

"She's very good."

"Thank you. I'll pass along the compliment."

The phone rang, and Cindi answered.

"Turner Investigations. How may I help you?"

Nicholas smiled.

"Just one moment, sir, and I'll see if he's in." Cindi put the phone on hold and spoke to Nicholas. "Sir, Joey Justice is on the line for you. Are you in?"

"Of course. I'll take the call."

Cindi punched the line on the phone again. "Please hold for Mr. Turner, sir." She again placed the line on hold.

Nicholas picked up his phone and punched the line. "Hello, Joey! How are you?"

"Hi, Nicholas. Not too good, I'm afraid."

"What's going on?"

Nicholas could hear Joey take a deep breath. "Marcus Moore asked me to call you, but I'd rather not get into the problem over the phone. Can you come to the Justice Security building right away? It's urgent, and I was told to offer a thousand dollars a day, plus expenses."

"Wow. That *is* urgent! Marcus must be desperate."

"It's a desperate situation, Nicholas. Can you come?"

"I'm on my way."

"Thanks, Nicholas. See you soon."

Nicholas hung up the phone as he stood. He reached into his bottom desk drawer, drew out his .357 Taurus revolver, checked to make sure that it was loaded, and put the gun into his shoulder holster.

"Something, sir?" asked Cindi.

"Yes, Cindi. Something urgent at the Justice Security building, and the FBI is involved. If you need anything, you can reach me there...or on my cell." He paused at the door and turned back. "Ummm...stick around until one o'clock or so, and you can lock up and take off. From the sound of it, I won't be back today."

"Yes, sir."

"I'll see you in the morning, Cindi. Thank you." He left the office.

Cindi frowned deeply.

MADELINE, ARE YOU WITH me? thought Nicholas.

I'm watching over Karen in school right now, Daddy.

Can you come?

Sure!

"Hi, Daddy!" said Madeline, suddenly appearing beside Nicholas, matching his brisk pace.

"Hi, sweetpea," said Nicholas. "I think I'm going to need you with me today...I was just called to Justice Security, and I don't know why. But, Marcus told them to call me in, so it must have something to do with children. I'll feel better if you're with me." He glanced to his side, but Madeline wasn't there. She had stopped walking a few steps behind him.

Madeline had a dreamy, faraway look on her face, tinged with fear.

"Madeline? What's wrong, sweetpea?" Nicholas walked back to Madeline, and started to take her hand...but his hand passed right through her. She had not physically materialized with him, so Nicholas was the only person that could see her.

Reciting, as if by rote, Madeline said, "When it's offered, you're supposed to take it."

Nicholas, puzzled, said, "Offered what, Madeline?"

"When it's offered, you're supposed to take it."

"Madeline!" said Nicholas sharply.

Madeline jumped, startled. She looked up at her father, fear etched in her face "Oh, Daddy, I'm so scared! I think this is the thing I've been worrying about!"

Nicholas knelt down to look into his daughter's eyes. "What are you talking about, sweetpea?"

"I was told that something *big* was coming...something *really* big. And I was told that you would be in the middle of it, and that you may not live through it. I was also told that..." Madeline didn't finish the sentence.

Nicholas said, "What else, Madeline?"

"Daddy, I may not survive this big thing, either."

Nicholas looked into his daughter's frightened eyes. "Honey, are you *sure* that this is the big something?"

Madeline looked down at her hands. "No, Daddy. They wouldn't tell me *when* it was going to happen." She looked back up at her father. "But, Daddy, Justice Security wouldn't call you unless it was something big! I am *so* scared!"

Inside, Nicholas turned cold. He could understand giving his own life during a case...but what could possibly threaten an *angel?*

Outwardly, he smiled reassuringly to his daughter. "Madeline, the chances of this being 'the big something' are probably pretty slim."

"But have you ever been called to help Justice Security before?"

Nicholas shook his head. "No, I haven't. They've referred cases to me, and I've referred some to them...and we both have Marcus Moore."

"Then this is *big*, Daddy...isn't it?"

"Yes, I guess it is, sweetpea. But it *still* may not be what you're so afraid of."

"Oh, Daddy, I hope not."

Nicholas stood and looked down at his daughter. "And even if it *is* the 'big something', you know how I feel about it. If I die doing good things, then it's worth it."

"Yes, Daddy."

Smiling, he said, "So...we good to go?"

Madeline took a deep breath. "If you say so, Daddy."

"That's my girl!"

Chapter 4

When Nicholas arrived at the Justice Security building, he parked his car in an empty slot across the street. He crossed the street, and entered the lobby of the building.

A sharply dressed, alert uniformed guard was behind the reception desk, talking to another uniformed guard. Nicholas had met Tony Armstrong twice before, and had heard of Tony's heroics during the incident at the *Wham!* night club.

Tony smiled and nodded at Nicholas, then finished what he was saying to the second guard. The other guard said, "Yes, sir!", then scurried away to do what Tony had ordered.

Tony held out his hand to Nicholas. "Hello, Mr. Turner! It's really good to see you again!"

Nicholas shook Tony's hand as he replied. "It's good to see you, too, Tony. And it's 'Nicholas', please. Mr. Turner was my dad."

"Sure thing, Nicholas," replied Tony. "They're expecting you upstairs. Would you come with me, please?"

The two men walked over to the elevators, and Tony pressed the "up" button.

"Tony, can you tell me anything about why I've been called here?" asked Nicholas.

Tony nodded. "I could, Nicholas, but they would only tell you all over again up on the fourth floor."

"You're probably right, of course," said Nicholas.

They rode in silence in the elevator.

When the elevator opened, Tony led the way.

Turk was sitting behind the desk that faced the elevators, one hand on the flat semi-automatic handgun that was inside a holster bolted to the underside of the desk. Tony knew the gun was there, but Nicholas did not.

Turk's hand remained on the weapon until Tony spoke.

"Turk Wendell, I'd like you to meet Nicholas Turner," said Tony.

The big man recognized the name, removed his hand from the weapon, and held his hand out to shake hands.

"Meetcha," said Turk.

"My pleasure," said Nicholas.

"Turk here is the executive flunky...I mean, secretary," said Tony, winking at Nicholas.

Nicholas nodded. "I see. I just hired a flunky...I mean, a secretary...myself. Do you enjoy the work?"

Turk nodded once.

"You have to forgive Turk. He doesn't talk very much," said Tony, as they walked toward the situation room. Winking again at Nicholas, he said, "His mother says he's special that way."

Both men heard Turk say, "Eat me, you whitebread bastard!"

"But I don't *like* watermelon, Turk!" said Tony.

Nicholas looked shocked at this exchange.

Both Tony and Turk burst out laughing.

"Oh, my God, Turk!" said Tony, between bursts of laughing "Did you see the look on his face?"

To Nicholas, Turk said, "Man, you shoulda seen yourself! You looked like you were about to shit a brick!"

"Turk and I are really good friends, Nicholas," explained Tony "We do this a lot to people that don't know one of us. Sorry."

"No, don't be sorry," said Nicholas. "I thought you two were about to start a world war there for a minute."

"Tony!" came a voice from inside the situation room.

"Yes, sir!" replied Tony sharply.

"Are you and Turk tormenting somebody out there again?"

Smiling, Tony replied, "Yes, sir!"

"Knock it off, and bring whoever it is in here!" A brief pause. "And don't forget the cavity search!"

"Yes, sir!" replied Tony. To Turk, he said, "Do you have those silicone gloves, Turk?"

"Right here," replied Turk, opening a desk drawer.

Nicholas was wide-eyed in surprise. "*No*-body is searching any of my cavities," he said firmly.

Laughter from several people could be heard from the situation room. When the sound came to them, both Turk and Tony started laughing, too.

Joey came out of the situation room and into the reception area. He held out his hand to Nicholas, who shook it.

Nicholas started nodding. "I get it! It's a joke, right?"

Joey started laughing again, and pointed to a point in the ceiling. "Yeah, Nicholas, we're pulling one on you. The camera is right there, and we were all watching you. Come say hello, and don't be mad at Tony or Turk."

"Oh, I'm not mad, Joey. I love a good joke, even if I'm the butt of it!"

I like them, Daddy. Nicholas heard Madeline's thought pop into his head.

I like them, too, sweetpea, Nicholas thought back.

Joey led the way into the situation room "I believe you know everyone here, don't you, Nicholas?"

"Yes, I think so. I met Megan Beck on Christmas Eve, didn't I?"

"You did. Glad you remembered," answered Joey.

Nicholas had never seen the situation room, and he was very impressed. Monitors fully covered one wall, and a string of computers on small tables were along another wall. A table with breakfast items stood in front of the room's window, and two large 'smart' boards were side by side on another wall. Recessed panels were imbedded in several places around the circular conference table, and several landline phones were spread around, too. A ham radio setup, complete with encryption abilities, was also in the room.

"Wow," said Nicholas, impressed. "Marcus has told me about the situation room, but I had no idea it was this elaborate!"

Joey cocked his head to the right a bit, and said, "Really? What else has Marcus told you about our company?"

"Just the basics, Joey," said Marcus, as he walked into the room. Marcus Moore's hair was brown and wavy, and he stood at an even six feet. He had blue eyes, and he was in his mid-thirties. He had been promoted to the city's Section Chief after the incident with the nightclub, and had been instrumental in getting the contract done quickly that gave unofficial sanction to Justice Security in their pursuit of Esteban Fernandez. He worked closely with the security company, and was Nicholas Turner's best friend. "Nothing that falls into the 'secret' category." Marcus sat down at the conference table. "Although he does know that we went to Chicago, remember? I asked him to join us for that one, but he couldn't make it."

"I remember, Marcus," said Joey. He looked closely at Nicholas. "Nicholas, we were talking before you got here. We'd like to invite you to come work with us. On a permanent basis."

Nicholas leaned back in his chair. "Joey, I'm flattered. But I don't want to work for someone else."

Joey smiled. "No one said work *for* us. The terminology was work *with* us. We've messed around long enough. We'd like to offer you a partnership in Justice Security. We have seven partners. We need one more, and we want you." Joey looked around the table. "We talked to Marcus about it. He said that as long as you could still take the cases that involved children, that he thought you would take it. A partnership also offers living facilities, and includes your own office."

Daddy, remember what I told you! When it's offered, you're supposed to take it!

Madeline, are you sure?

Yes, Daddy. On this, I'm positive.

Nicholas shook his head in disbelief. "A partnership. I wasn't expecting that. Well, if I can call Meredith, and if she says okay, then I'll be glad to be your partner."

Everyone at the table began applauding.

"'Bout damn time!" said Louie "We been needin' some new thinkin' around here!"

"I'm certainly glad to see it happen," said Jessica. "Perhaps you're not as dense as some of my *other* partners."

"Congratulations, Nicky," said Marcus. "That means I'll get to work with you a lot more than I do now."

Joey, smiling, said, "Nick, I'll have the papers drawn up within the hour." He held out his hand. "Welcome aboard!"

Yayyy, Daddy!

A voice from the door interrupted them. "Excuse me! Marcus, did you forget something?"

Everyone turned Tony was standing in the door.

"I found it wandering around the lobby. It looked lost, so I thought it might find a home up here." Tony looked behind him, and made a 'come on' motion.

Tory Masterson walked into the situation room.

Tory was the new FBI agent in town, under the able tutelage of Marcus. Tory had been a Detective First Class in Chicago, and, because of his help in fighting Esteban Fernandez, had been offered a position in the city's FBI office by Marcus. Tory had jumped at the chance, and he and his family had moved to the city from Chicago...after Tory had made it through Quantico. Marcus had chosen Tory to be his second-in-charge for all things Justice Security.

"Aw, crap, I forgot about Tory," said Marcus. "Sorry, Tory."

"No problem," replied Tory, pulling up a chair to the conference table.

"Okay, let's run down the situation for Nicky and Tory," said Marcus. "This morning, a group of people kidnapped a busload of children and the bus driver. They have disappeared with them. Joey received a phone call from a man that calls himself Gary McGee. He said that he was the leader of the kidnappers. This McGee also called Channel 7 News this morning, and told Miriam Apple that he had kidnapped the children. He said that the children and the driver were in a secure location, and that it was booby-trapped with explosives, and set with a timer. McGee said that he would trade the safety of the children for Joey Justice, so that McGee could turn him over to Esteban Fernandez for the bounty on Joey's head. You with us so far?"

Nicholas, whose eyes had become wider with each statement, said, "Yeah, I'm with you! Incredible!"

"Tell us about it, Nick," said Joey. "Even though Fernandez isn't personally behind this, he's still the reason for it. But, we'll fill you in on all of that later."

Marcus continued, "Of course, Joey told him to basically stuff himself, but the clock is ticking. We have to find the kidnappers and the children, and we have to do it by five this afternoon. Or, according to McGee, the children and the driver will die." Marcus looked at his best friend. "I wanted you on this one for two reasons, Nicky. One, you usually can get good intel fast, and, two...well, you know what number two is."

"Marcus, you don't mean...," said Nicholas.

Marcus nodded.

"That's not something I'm prepared to make public knowledge, Marcus," said Nicholas. He was emphatic.

"Nicky, public knowledge is one thing. Your partners are another. Joey deserves to know. Especially since that's probably our only chance to find those children."

"And what happens when one of them spills the secret?" said Nicholas. He was becoming angry.

"Nick, please don't be angry. I don't know what your secret is, but I can guarantee you that no one in this room will ever disclose it without your permission," said Joey. "We're partners, and the only reason we haven't offered a partnership to Marcus, and even Tory, is because we actually need them to be FBI agents." He raised his hand. "Let me ask you a question, Nicholas. Has Marcus ever told you anything about our cases that weren't already public knowledge?"

Nicholas shook his head "No."

"That courtesy now extends to you. No, let me rephrase: that *requirement* now extends to you. We keep secrets very well in this organization."

Nicholas looked at the table for a minute, then looked at the faces around the table. "Do you have somewhere that I can be alone for a moment? I need to think about this. I won't be a minute, I promise."

Joey nodded. "Sure." He stood. "Come on, I'll show you to your office."

"My...wow," said Nicholas as he stood. "My office. In the Justice Security building. Incredible."

Joey led him out of the situation room, down the hall, and to an ornate wooden door. "This is your official office. Although, I might suggest another office, if you think Meredith will go for it. If, for some reason, you don't think my suggestion will suit you, this will be your permanent office."

"Thanks, Joey I won't be a minute. I just need to organize my thoughts."

"I understand completely."

Joey walked back to the situation room.

Nicholas opened the door to the office. The room was tastefully decorated, but not elaborately. It had a good-sized mahogany desk, with a comfortable chair behind it. There was a couch and some comfortable chairs around a large coffee table. A computer monitor sat quietly on the right side of the desk, and the large window looked out on a very nice view of the small grassy area on the south side of the building. Nondescript paintings hung on the walls, but they obviously could be replaced. A choice of lighting was available, from small table and floor lamps to overhead fluorescents and track lighting.

Nicholas was impressed.

"This is nice, Daddy," said Madeline. She had appeared beside him.

"It is, isn't it?" replied Nicholas. He squatted down beside her. "Maddie, I'm not sure that I'm ready to tell them about you. Do you have any advice?"

"Just one thing, Daddy," said the little girl. "You're s'posed to." She paused. "But the choice is yours." She shrugged. "I'm s'posed to remind you that you have free will, and if you don't want to tell them about me, you don't have to. But you're s'posed to."

Nicholas shook his head at himself. He knew that if he was going to be partners with these people, he had to tell them about Madeline. *Maybe she's supposed to help them, too.*

"Maybe so, Daddy," said Madeline, reading his thought. "Nobody's told me."

"Okay, then, sweetpea. Let's go."

WHEN JOEY CAME BACK into the room, he said to Marcus, "Okay, what is the big secret, Marcus?"

"It's not mine to tell, Joe," replied Marcus. "It's big enough that it has to come from Nicky, or not at all."

"I have a feeling about it," said Megan. "I think I know what it is."

Dexter looked at his wife. "What is it, sweet wife?"

Megan shook her head. "I'll tell everyone if what I'm thinking is right." She abruptly leaned over and whispered into Dexter's ear.

Dexter looked perplexed. "No way!"

"Not a word, Dexter Beck!" said Megan sternly. "If that's it, I just wanted someone to know what I was thinking."

"It couldn't be, Megan," said Dexter.

Megan gave her husband a look. "Shut *up*, Dexter."

"Okay, I'm the new kid on the block," said Tory. "And I'm as lost as last year's Easter egg."

Marcus reflected for a moment. "Tory, it might be best if you headed out to Sardis County. Take your family. Buy, or rent, a place. You might not want to be here for this one."

"Now, Marcus?" asked Tory.

Marcus started to say something, but stopped.

Nicholas came into the room, and stopped just inside the door. "Okay, apparently I'm supposed to tell you my big secret." The look on his face was resigned. "I don't know why, but I've learned not to question. Ladies and gentlemen, I'd like you to meet my daughter, Madeline."

Madeline came into the room, and stood beside her father.

Both Joey's and Megan's eyes widened.

"*You!*" said Megan.

"Hey, kid!" said Marcus.

Joey was smiling. "I've seen you, haven't I? You were at Jennie Lou's funeral, weren't you?"

Madeline nodded. "Hi, Joey. Hi, Megan."

Nicholas looked at Madeline. "You know them, Maddie?"

"Yes, Daddy."

"How do you know them, honey?" asked Nicholas, with a puzzled look on his face.

"When Joey saw me, I was at that funeral to comfort the kids, and to comfort Joey through them. I saw Megan at the church this past Christmas. I was s'posed to give her some faith and hope." She looked at Megan. "Did I do it?"

Megan smiled and nodded. "Yes, hon, you did. You've made it even stronger today." Megan turned and hit Dexter on the arm. "I *told* you I saw a second little girl at the church!"

Dexter was amazed. All he could say was, "Megan was right. I don't believe it."

Louie lost patience. "Okay, you guys know this girl. Great. Who the hell is she, besides being Nicky's daughter?"

Madeline turned her gaze to the big man. The depth and warmth inside her eyes immediately calmed Louie, and he felt a great inner peace. Madeline walked to him and said, "Percival, you've been having some awful nightmares, haven't you?"

Unable to speak, Louie only nodded.

"I'm sorry, but I can't do anything about them. It has to come from inside you. You're fighting with yourself, you know."

Louie said, "Thank you, honey." He reached for her hand, but his hand passed through hers. He recoiled away from her. With wide eyes, he said, "She's a damn *ghost!* What the *hell?*"

Nicholas stepped closer. "Not a ghost, Louie."

Agitated, Louie said, "Then what the hell is she?"

"Show them, Madeline."

Madeline nodded, then closed her eyes. Slowly, she transformed into her 'angel' form. She glowed with an inner white light, and pure, white power cascaded from her shoulders, giving the appearance of wings. Her brown hair blew slightly, as if in a breeze, and her expression showed both maturity and knowledge. She was obviously still Madeline, a ten-year-old child, but she was also more than that. She was breathtakingly beautiful.

"I'm what you might call an 'angel,'" said Madeline.

Chapter 5

"**H**oly *shit!*" said Louie.

"So this is the big secret about Nicholas," Joey said to Marcus. "No wonder you kept it to yourself."

Dexter was dumbfounded. He had always held a small piece of doubt inside as to whether there was a Heaven, but to have its existence confirmed so quickly and so intensely was mind-blowing to him.

Jessica was smiling from ear to ear, as was Misty.

There was silence for a few moments as they all stared at Madeline, and contemplated what her very existence meant to their beliefs, when the silence was abruptly broken by Tory Masterson.

"I'm sorry, people, everything today may be commonplace here, but I *don't understand what's going on!* And I would *appreciate* it if someone would tell me!"

Nicholas, still in awe of his daughter's transformation, even though he'd seen it many times, finally answered. "When my daughter was conceived, an angel had chosen to be reborn as a human, and had chosen my daughter to be that human life. Apparently, from time to time, angels choose to do that, to remind themselves what being human is all about. But, my first wife, Janie, miscarried our daughter because of the rampaging cancer that killed her just a few weeks later.

"Madeline, however, had chosen to age as a real little girl would age, and spent ten years in what we call 'Heaven'...with Janie.

"Recently, during that big case I solved about the kidnap-to-orders that were going on with the corrupt police officers, Madeline chose to appear to me for two reasons. One, because I needed help with the case, and, two, that the woman that hired me was supposed to be my second chance at love. Madeline also chose to stay on earth with me, to live with her father for a while. She's been helping me ever since."

Nicholas looked around the room. "So, yes, Madeline is my daughter. She is also an angel. And she answers to another father as well as me. When she tells me that I'm supposed to do something, I do it. Not because she tells me to, but because her other father has told her that I need to. I have freedom of choice, and can refuse anything I'm supposed to do, but I don't usually exercise that choice, unless I feel that there's a strong chance that Madeline would be hurt.

"And she can be hurt, if she's in her physical form...her 'real' self, as we call it. She can even be killed in that form, so we avoid it when we can. She and I can communicate telepathically, and she has the power to transport people, as well as herself, from one point to another with the speed of thought. She can transform into her physical self, take hold of something in our physical world, and 'fade' it back into her realm, so that it appears solid, but your hand would pass right through it, just like Louie's hand passed through Madeline's. She also has some serious power that is not of this world, and can zap someone that is evil with a huge jolt." Nicholas paused while he thought. "I think that's...no, wait, she can also take people to a higher plane of existence, and show that person what they can't see in human form. I think that's everything."

Nicholas took a breath. "This morning, as I was leaving my office to come over here, Madeline sort of 'tranced', and said, 'When it's offered, you should take it.' She reminded me of that when you offered me the partnership."

"I don't know why Daddy is supposed to take the partnership. I just know that he is," said Madeline, in a much more mature, adult voice.

"Oh, yeah, that's something else," said Nicholas "When she's in that form, she the combination of her human DNA and her angel self. She's more than a little girl."

"Does all of this mean she can see the future?" asked Louie.

"She can, and she can't," answered Nicholas. "She can, if her other father lets her. Otherwise, she's as blind about it as we are. She asks often, which is why she's able to help me, but the answers are often hard to figure out. They're meant to be that way, so that we can choose our own paths."

"I can see what I'm meant to see, Louie. No more and no less," said Madeline. "Just as I was able to see your nightmares. But, I can't do anything but sympathize, because that's all I'm able to do. But, I can tell you this, Louie: you will have to use all of your strength for today's events. Physical, mental, and emotional strength...you will need them all."

Madeline turned to Jessica. "You are also facing nightmares, Jessica, along with the fear of being a jinx and a failure. You are neither. You are the soul and the conscience of this group. Your strength has overcome much adversity, and you should never doubt yourself. The nightmares will pass, although not in the way you expect."

Jessica's eyes widened, and her hand unconsciously went to her chest, covering her heart.

Madeline turned to Dexter. "Dexter, you are the representation of peace and patience, but you will be tested today, and tested harshly. It may seem unfair, but it is what is meant to be. That is all I can say, because that is all I know."

The angel turned to Megan. "Megan, you have a huge heart, full of love for your husband and your friends. You, above all others, will be tested today, and the advice I gave you inside St. Francis's church remains the same: Be strong, and do not lose yourself. And remember that I wish there were another way."

Tory was now the focus of Madeline's warm gaze. "Tory Masterson. You are new to this dynamic group of people. You have the advantage of a young man's thinking and abilities. You can do well with these people, if you hold your ambitions in check. Enjoy these people. They will teach you all you need to know."

When Madeline turned to Misty, the woman said to the little girl, "Madeline, if you don't mind, I'd rather not know anything."

Madeline smiled at Misty, nodded, and turned to Joey.

Joey said, "I'm not sure that I want to hear anything, either."

"But you will. You're supposed to." Madeline seemed to stand taller as she addressed Joey. "You have a strength and determination that these people rely on. If you begin to doubt yourself, you have lost your battle. Retain the knowledge that nothing is as dismal and as absent of hope as you think. If you remember that, Joey, you can conquer any adversity in this lifetime." Madeline took a step closer. "Her love for you is eternal. She is your soulmate, Joey Justice. Do not forget that."

Marcus had never seen Madeline in this form. Nicholas had described it to him often, but he was seeing her true self for the first time. When she turned to him, Marcus said, "Hello again, kid."

Madeline studied Marcus. She looked deep into his eyes, almost as if she were studying his soul. When she completed her study, she smiled a broad, warm smile. "Marcus Moore. You needn't worry. Things will work out the way they are supposed to. Show no fear. And leave time to love."

Madeline looked around at everyone one more time. "And that is all that my father wanted me to tell you. I hope it helps you and gives you comfort." She closed her eyes and concentrated. As the group watched, Madeline became a little girl again.

"That's my big secret, Joey," said Nicholas. "You guys sure you still want me as a partner?"

Joey looked around the table at his friends, then stood up. "Nicholas, we would be honored if you would join us."

And that was that.

I'D SURE LIKE TO KNOW where the hell I am, thought Snickers. *I can't see nuthin'.*

Snickers tried to move his arms, and couldn't. He felt the rope and the duct tape, and realized that he wouldn't be moving his arms anytime soon. At least they hadn't cut off his circulation.

He wasn't blindfolded. He wasn't gagged.

Wherever he was, it was as dark as could be.

The last thing Snickers remembered was Cindi telling him that this was for his own good, and that it might prevent something terrible from happening. He didn't remember anything after that...she must have knocked him out somehow.

Jeez, what a stupid thing for me to do. I never should have followed that chick.

Snickers struggled against the ropes and the tape one more time, then settled back.

Shit. I wish I had some way of knowing what time it is. I'm hungry, too.

He pulled against the ropes again.

Dammit!

"OKAY, IT'S ELEVEN-FIFTEEN. We don't have a lot of time. Nicholas, we have our people scattered out, trying to find out where the kidnappers or the children might be. We're hitting up every informant on our payroll, but, so far, nothing," said Joey. "Do you have any informants?"

Nicholas nodded. "I have several. I use the working girls in Hooker Hollow a lot, but my best informant is a guy named Snickers."

"So, he's good?" asked Joey.

"He's very good. I have no idea how he keeps his finger on everything," replied Nicholas.

"I've used him," said Jim. "He's great with computers, too."

"Is he a bad guy?" asked Dexter.

Nicholas shook his head. "No, not at all. He used to be a druggie, but he's been a good informant...a good *friend*...since my cop days. He works as a computer programmer, and hangs around a lot at McFeelMe's. Let me give him a call."

ALICE MARSHALL WAS trying her best to keep the children entertained.

Alice was the driver of the school bus that had been captured by the kidnappers that morning. They had come aboard the bus, put a gun to her head, and told the children that they would kill her if they didn't stay quiet and do what they were told.

The children, ranging in age from five to fifteen, had all kept quiet. The older children had helped to keep the younger ones calm, for which Alice was very grateful.

They had all been herded into this place. The kidnapper that spoke to them was short, and had a deep Southern drawl.

"Now, ya'll need to realize that unless our demands are met, the explosives that you see all around the top of this room will go off at five o'clock." He pointed to a timer that was counting down the remaining time. "When that counter hits zero, it'll trigger the explosion. If you tamper with any of it, it will explode, and if anyone tampers with it from outside, it will explode. So, unless you kids want to die, leave that stuff alone."

The kidnappers had left, giving them bottles of water and a flashlight, and locked them inside.

The children had been full of questions at the beginning, but had finally fallen quiet. Some of them were sleeping, and the older ones were looking around, trying to see if the kidnappers had overlooked a way for them all to escape.

There was none.

Everyone was on the floor. The flashlight was off to save the batteries, and the only illumination they had was being emitted from the red numbers that were counting down.

They had less than six hours.

DEXTER AND MEGAN WERE checking the internet for references to Gary McGee. Joey, Louie, and Marcus were filling Tory in on some of the things that he needed to know about working with Justice Security as an FBI liaison, while Jim listened in. Misty and Jessica were chatting quietly with Madeline, while Nicholas tried to reach Snickers.

"What is the afterlife like, Madeline?" asked Misty.

Madeline smiled. "It's made up to be whatever the best thing you ever wanted to have. Everybody has their own ideas, and they come true."

"Are you stuck with that idea throughout eternity?" asked Jessica.

Madeline smiled and shook her head. "No. If you want to change it all, you can. All you have to do is think it, and it happens."

"Why did you appear at the cemetery during Jennie Lou's funeral, Madeline?" asked Misty. "Joey told me that Phillip was given a gift to prove you had been there, and that he was able to speak clearly for a few moments."

Madeline nodded. "Yes, that was Phillip's gift. And Joey's, too. I wanted to give Joey a little bit of comfort after he lost Jennie Lou, and to let him know that she was in good hands."

"I know that he grieved for her, but he didn't dwell on her death as much as he would have if you hadn't appeared that day. He was so amazed that an angel would take an interest in him that he walked around here for several days with a big smile on his face."

With a smile, Madeline said, "Good. And Phillip was able to tell the other children how much he loved them, and how much he loved Jackie, and how much he missed Jennie Lou. It was a good gift all around."

Nicholas slammed the receiver down on the landline phone.

"I can't find Snickers," said Nicholas. "I called him at work, and they said that they hadn't seen him since yesterday. He left work at lunch with some vacation time, because he came to help me hang pictures at my office. He left the office when I started talking to the girl that I hired to work for me part-time, and he hasn't been seen since. I called Hank McFeely to see if Snickers had been there, but Hank hasn't seen Snick since the night before last." Nicholas stared off into space. "I'm worried about the little turd."

Jessica asked, "Can we help, Nicholas?"

Nicholas shook his head. "Thank you, Jessica, but if I can't find him, he doesn't want to be found." Then he smiled. "But I know someone that *can* find him." He looked at Madeline.

Madeline smiled back. "Sure, Daddy I'll find him." She closed her eyes, and winked out of sight.

"Oh, my *God!*" said Jessica. "How did you get used to that, Nicholas?"

"It wasn't easy. She still surprises me sometimes."

Madeline winked back in. She had a frightened look on her face.

"I found him, Daddy, but something was trying to keep me from him," said the little girl. "I don't know what it was, but it scared me."

"Are you okay, sweetpea?" asked Nicholas.

"Oh, I'm fine, Daddy. But Snickers is in darkness. He's tied up, and taped up, and he can't see anything."

"Does someone have a flashlight that I can borrow?" said Nicholas, standing up.

Dexter tossed a flashlight to Nicholas.

"Mind if I come with you?" asked Joey.

"Madeline, can you take both of us to Snickers?" asked Nicholas.

"Sure, Daddy. No problem."

"Then do it." said Nicholas.

Madeline closed her eyes to concentrate, and became solid. She reached out and took a hand from each man.

"Joey, there's no way I can prepare you for this experience. In our realm, it happens in the wink of an eye...but it will seem like several minutes for you," said Nicholas.

"I'm ready," said Joey.

"Close your eyes," said Madeline.

Both men closed their eyes.

Madeline closed her eyes again.

A bright, white glow surrounded the three, and, as the people in the Justice Security situation room watched, Joey Justice winked out of sight, along with Nicholas Turner, and his daughter Madeline.

Chapter 6

Joey felt warmth, love, and concern flowing from his friends in the situation room.

"Joey, you can open your eyes now," said Madeline.

Joey opened his eyes to a world of light. He drew in a quick breath. Everything around him shone with light in a plethora of bright colors. The desks, the computers, the monitors on the wall all shone bright pale blue. He could see Misty, Louie, and the others, and they were all surrounded by a white glow that gradually changed to a thick pale yellow band, then a dark blue as it grew closer to their bodies. Orbs of light of all colors imaginable passed in and out of the room, and went through walls as if the walls weren't there. Occasionally, a figure recognizable as human would pass through going up or down. He noticed that the ones moving upward were surrounded by bright colors, and the ones moving downward were shining in extremely dark colors. It was more beautiful than he could ever hope to describe. Then he looked at Madeline.

She was still Madeline, but she was surrounded by a pale white glow. From the point where her shoulders met the base of her neck, bright white light cascaded to the left and the right all the way to the floor. The cascading lights were not wings, but looked remarkably like them. The blue in her eyes glowed with an intensity that normally would have hurt his eyes to see.

"Joey, I want you to look at the aura surrounding Misty, and I'll explain what you're seeing," said Madeline.

Joey looked at Misty, and drew in another sharp breath when he saw the intensity of the colors in her aura.

"The outside whiteness is her goodness. See how wide it is? That means she's a good person. The wide yellow band is her love for you, and your friends – Jessica, Louie, Dexter, Megan, and everyone else. The dark blue closest to her body is her worry. She's worried for you, and for all of us."

She gestured to the room. "Everything has an aura around it, even things like a desk or a soda can. Everything in here has a pale blue light to it, because you use them to do good things.

"The orbs you see passing through are messengers. I had to explain this to Daddy the first time I brought him to this plane. The orbs are not quite what you call 'angels', but they're close. They pass messages from those in charge to people that are doing their work here on earth. Random acts of kindness often result from a brush with one of them. The brighter the color, the more goodness is contained in the message. Try not to interfere with a dark-colored orb, though. They obviously serve a darker power. They can cause random acts of violence and horror if you accidentally touch one."

Joey indicated the lights cascading from her shoulders. "What are those, Madeline? Are they wings?"

"Those represent my energy and life force. Look at Daddy's shoulders, then look at your own."

Joey looked at the lights cascading from Nicholas' shoulders. When he looked at his own, he had the same cascading power flowing from his shoulders.

"Don't panic, Joey, we're not angels," said Nicholas. "Madeline says that if we continue to do good things, that we have the potential to become them."

"We're not speaking," observed Joey. "We're communicating telepathically, aren't we?"

Madeline smiled. "Very good, Joey. Yes, we are."

A human-like figure passed through the office, moving diagonally upwards, bathed in a pale yellow light.

"What are the human figures passing through here, Madeline?"

"What do you think they are?"

"I think they're...people that have just died, and are on their way to where you came from."

"Very good, but not all are going to the good. Remember that the darker colored orbs serve another power? It's the same way with those that have died. If they're surrounded by a dark color, they're going somewhere else."

"Joey, have you noticed the maturity in Madeline's voice?" asked Nicholas.

Joey nodded. "Why is that?"

"Here, she's more angel than little girl," said Nicholas "She chose this, and was cheated out of a full life as a human. We all have freedom of choice, including angels. Our maker wouldn't have it any other way."

Joey felt that he could watch the orbs and colors and human shapes forever, if he didn't have some children to save. "May I ask you something, Madeline?"

"Of course."

"When you spoke to Dexter and Megan, you said something about a 'test'. What did you mean?"

"I truly don't know, Joey. I told them what I was instructed to tell them, and that was all I knew," replied Madeline.

"That scares me."

"As it does me." Madeline looked at the two men. "Now, shall we go save Snickers?"

"Yes," both men thought in unison.

They winked abruptly into total darkness.

"Who's there?"

"Snickers?"

"Nicky? Is that you?"

Nicholas clicked on the flashlight, careful to aim the bright light toward the ceiling so that he wouldn't blind his friend.

"Yeah, it's me, Snick," said Nicholas.

"Who's that with ya?" Snickers asked. There was some worry in his voice.

"I brought Joey Justice, and someone you haven't met yet," replied Nicholas.

"You didn't, you know, bring that Cindi girl, did you?" asked Snickers.

"No, why?"

"She's the one that, you know, put me here."

Nicholas had been examining the ropes that had been used to tie Snickers to the chair he was sitting in. He stopped, and looked at Snickers.

"Are you serious? *Cindi* did this?"

"Yeah! I, you know, followed her yesterday when she left, you know, your office. I lost her, and, you know, next thing I know, I'm here, and she's, you know, telling me that she's trying to stop something, you know, bad from happening." Snickers looked at Joey. "Nice to meecha, Mr. Justice. I've heard a lot of, you know, good things about you."

Joey smiled at Snickers. "Same here, Snickers. Hank McFeely speaks very highly of you. He says you're a trustworthy man. And Jim Dandy has nothing but high praise for you."

"Well, you know, I do what I can...especially for Nicky."

"He's telling the truth, Daddy," Madeline said to Nicholas.

"*Daddy?*" said Snickers. He saw Madeline peeking out from behind Nicholas. "You got something you want to, you know, tell me, Nicky?"

"Yeah. Snickers, meet my daughter, Madeline. Sorry you had to meet her this way." Nicholas looked up in disgust. "Joey, I can't find a knot in this rope. It's like it was made around him somehow! Do you have a pocket knife on you?"

"No. Normally, I have one in a sheath down my back, but I wasn't prepared for combat today."

Nicholas sighed. "Okay, we do it the hard way. Madeline, can you fade all of us out of here?"

"Well, of *course* I can, Daddy!" replied the little girl. "Stop being silly!"

Madeline moved until she was standing in front of Snickers. He looked at her curiously.

"What did he mean by, you know, 'fade'?" he asked.

Madeline smiled, and put her hands on his shoulders. "You're about to find out, Snickers. Daddy, Joey, I need you both to put a hand on my shoulder."

The two men each put a hand on one of Madeline's shoulders.

"Watch my eyes, Snickers," said Madeline. "You'll be fine."

"Why? What's gonna, you know...oh, holy *shit*!"

As they winked out of sight, the rope and tape that had held Snickers collapsed onto the floor.

Chapter 7

Three men and a little girl suddenly winked into existence inside the situation room at Justice Security.

"Oh, my *God!*" said Snickers. "Somebody please tell me, you know, what's goin' on?" He curled up into a fetal position on the floor. "Please, Nicky, tell me! Please!" He was so stressed that he didn't even say, 'you know'.

"Let me, Daddy," said Madeline. "It's a shock for him." She sat down on the floor next to the shaking, scared man. "Snickers, look at me."

"N-no!"

"Why?"

"'Cause you can't be real!"

"What makes you think that I'm not real?"

"You're an *angel*, for Chrissake!"

"What's wrong with being an angel?" asked Madeline gently.

Snickers had covered his face with his hands. He mumbled something.

"What did you say?" asked Madeline.

Snickers took his hands away from his mouth and said, "I said, 'I'm not worthy'!"

Madeline reached out and touched the shivering man on the shoulder. He flinched from her touch. "Snickers, look at me."

"No!"

"*LOOK AT ME!*" Madeline's voice boomed, and seemed to come from everywhere.

Everyone's eyes widened. Louie stood straight up out of his chair, and Dexter jumped as if he had been poked. Tory and Megan were both staring with open mouths, and everyone else was startled.

Sniffing, with tears running down his face, Snickers looked at Madeline.

The little girl looked deeply into the man's eyes and said, "Although I am less than the least of all the Lord's people, this grace was given me."

Snickers, still sniffing, said, "Ephesians, chapter three, verse eight."

Madeline nodded "You have had many tests thrown into your path through this life, and yet you have overcome each one. In my Father's eyes, you are more worthy than many holy men, Walter Thompson. Now, stand, and help my daddy and his friends." She held out her hand to help Snickers stand up.

Snickers looked into her eyes, and only saw warmth and caring there. He reached up, took her hand, and stood.

Madeline impulsively gave the man a hug. He returned it.

"I gotta question, Nicky," said Snickers. "Where the hell am I?" Snickers didn't notice, but he wasn't saying 'you know' when he spoke. His nervousness was gone.

Nicholas, however, noticed.

"You are in the situation room on the fourth floor of the Justice Security building," said Nicholas. "Tell me about Cindi. Everything you can remember."

Snickers told them about everything leading up to his encounter with Cindi Moore, and everything after that he could remember.

"So, you don't know where you were, or how she got you there?" asked Joey.

"No."

"Joey, I'm gettin' mighty creeped out about all of this right now," said Louie. "This is spookier than dealing with Fernandez!"

"For once, I have to agree with Louie, Joey," added Jessica. "This is becoming far too...*ethereal*, I guess...for Justice Security."

"I'm not too sure what that word means," said Tory "But it's twelve-oh-five right now. We have less than five hours to find those kids."

"Right," said Nicholas. "Marcus, I know you wanted me in on this because of Madeline. Do you have any pictures of any of the children?"

Marcus, with his lips pressed together, shook his head.

"I got that," said Dexter. "Pictures of the kids and the bus driver, coming right up." Dexter's fingers flew across the keyboard of one of the computers, and, as they all watched, photos began popping up on each of the situation room's monitors.

Turk chose that moment to come into the room. He had a file folder in his hand.

"Boss," said the big man.

"Whatcha got, Turk?" asked Joey.

"Lawyers dropped off these papers. They said I had to use my notary stamp on it when Mr. Turner signs it."

Joey looked at Nicholas. "Do you want to do this now?"

"Umm...," said Nicholas. "I do, but I need to talk to Meredith first. May I? I promise that it won't take long."

Joey said, "Sure. I think we all need to have some lunch anyway. When you get back, can you meet us in the cafeteria? It's on the first floor."

Nicholas nodded. "Sure Madeline, will you take me home?"

"Sure, Daddy."

Nicholas turned to Snickers. "Snick, that man," he pointed at Marcus, "is Marcus Moore. We've talked about him. And this," he pointed at Joey, "is Joey Justice. I need you to stay with them until Madeline and I get back, okay? They'll take good care of you."

Snickers nodded. "I see Jim Dandy, too. That's good enough for me. And somebody needs to explain about you having a daughter, and why she's an angel, Nicky."

"I'll tell you all about it, Snickers," said Marcus. "As a matter of fact, I'll tell the whole thing to all of you during lunch. How's that?"

"Thank you, Marcus," said Nicholas. To Madeline, he said, "Okay, sweetpea, let's go home for a minute."

Madeline took her daddy's hand, closed her eyes, and, when the white glow surrounded both of them, they winked out.

"I have to say that I will *never* get used to that," said Jessica.

Turk was staring at the spot that had just held Nicholas and Madeline. He had no expression on his face, which wasn't unusual. His body was trembling all over. And that *was* unusual.

Louie, who had worked with Turk on field assignments for years, recognized that his friend was terrified. He slapped Turk on the back and said, "Come on, brother, the little girl's an angel. Come to the cafeteria, and Marcus will tell us all about it."

MEREDITH WAS IN HER studio, working on a painting commissioned by one of the city's Aldermen. It was a family portrait, and she was working from a series of photographs that she had taken of the Alderman's family.

And they are the most pretentious group of snobs I have ever met, she thought to herself.

The windows in Meredith's studio had a wonderful view of the back yard, and French doors that opened to the patio. She had the doors open, enjoying the just-right weather, and Karen was sitting in one of the patio chairs, reading a book on her tablet. Meredith and Nicholas had made the decision to home-school the girl, at least for a couple of years.

Just as Meredith applied the paint brush to the Alderman's face for his moustache, Madeline and Nicholas winked in right beside her. Startled, Meredith's hand jerked, and a dark line appeared under the brush across the Alderman's face...and his wife's.

"Nicholas, I have asked you not to do that!" said Meredith sternly.

With a sheepish grin, Nicholas said, "I'm sorry, honey."

Madeline said, "We're sorry, Meredith."

"Why on *earth* are you home so early?"

Karen came inside from the patio "I thought I heard voices in here!" She went to Nicholas and hugged him, then hugged Madeline.

"Sweetheart, we need to talk. It's important," said Nicholas.

Meredith was wiping the dark line from the faces of her clients, trying to remove it before the paint dried. "What is it, Nicholas?"

"Marcus called me in on the school bus kidnapping today."

"You mean the one with the kidnappers trying to trade with Justice Security?"

Nicholas nodded.

"What is so special about that?"

"Marcus wanted Madeline in on it."

Meredith put down her cloth. "I see."

"That's not all. When I arrived at the Justice Security building, I was offered a partnership in the company."

Meredith searched her husband's eyes. "And what did you tell them?"

"I said yes, but that I had to talk to you first."

Meredith had just picked up her brush again, but put it down and looked at her husband.

"Madeline had told me before we ever got there, that if it was offered, I was supposed to take it," said Nicholas. "I would still be able to work on my child cases, but I would have the entire company's resources to call on if I needed them. I would have an office there, and there are some nice apartments in the building for the partners...although I think Joey has something else in mind for us."

"What do you think, Nicholas? We could just pack up our angel and move there?" She looked at her husband's face. "You've already told them about her, haven't you?"

"Yes, I did," replied Nicholas.

"Do you realize what you have...," began Meredith.

"Meredith, stop," said Madeline.

Meredith looked at the child "What did you say?"

"I said, 'stop'. Daddy was supposed to introduce me to them, and he's supposed to take this partnership. He's doing everything that my father has asked of him."

Meredith sighed. "Nicholas, being part of Justice Security is dangerous. From what I have seen on the news, it is dangerous just being around them."

"And I remind you that a dirty cop kidnapped Karen. Danger is everywhere, honey. But, this is an opportunity that I can't pass up."

Meredith looked at her painting for a moment. "Would we *have* to live in the building? I mean, could we please keep our house?"

Nicholas took her hands in his. "Of course we can keep our house! It's ours, free and clear. We'd be fools to get rid of it."

"What about Karen? Will she be safe there? And my studio! Would I have space there, or would I have to go out to paint?"

Nicholas shook his head. "Those are questions that I can't answer, because I don't know the answers." His face lit up. "Hey, why don't you and Karen come back there with us? You can ask questions, you can get the tour of the place, and Madeline and I can help find those poor kids!"

Meredith looked at Karen. Karen nodded.

"Very well. We will all go back," said Meredith.

Madeline smiled. "Hold hands, everybody!"

IN THE CAFETERIA, MARCUS had explained everything he knew about Madeline, and her appearance in his friend's life, to Turk, Snickers, and the partners of Justice Security.

The group was seated at a huge round table in the corner of the cafeteria. No other employees were seated close by, and the cafeteria workers were cleaning up and preparing that night's dinner. Justice Security's cafeteria was staffed and open twenty-four hours a day, because of the schedules that both the grunts and the plainclothes people worked. Joey believed in having free food available for any employee that was working busy shifts, or if they were just having a little "tight with money" period.

"A good security officer is one that doesn't have to worry about where his next meal is coming from," Joey had said many times. "We don't get a lot of lucky breaks in this business, but I can damn sure keep my people fed."

Marcus was looking at Joey while he made a point.

"Nicholas would not have been able to break up that kidnapping ring without Madeline's help," he told them. "He told me that Madeline had used her power bolts to just about fry George Parker! And when she's mad, look out – the wind starts blowing, and you know that little sound burst that she gave to Snickers? That's nothing compared to her full-blast 'angel voice'! I've heard it, and it really booms!"

"What are her power bolts?" asked Misty.

"Well, they're...," he started, but stopped as he looked toward the door. "I have a better idea. Why not ask the young lady directly?" Marcus pointed. "The Turners have arrived."

Marcus, Joey, and Misty stood, and walked over to Nicholas and his family.

"Joey Justice, Misty Wilhite, I'd like you to meet my wife, Meredith, and my almost-daughter, Karen," said Nicholas. "We all consider Karen to be my daughter, but we're just waiting for the adoption papers to be signed by the judge."

"I might be able to help some with that," said Joey. "Who's the judge?"

"Judge Edith Stone."

Joey nodded and smiled. "I'll call her tomorrow. You'll have the signed papers by tomorrow afternoon...provided we're all still here then."

Misty turned to Meredith. "Oh, Meredith, I'm so glad to meet you! Marcus talks about you all the time, but I was beginning to think we'd never get to meet you!"

"It is a pleasure to be here, Misty," said Meredith. "I was surprised when Nicholas told me about the partnership, and the fact that living facilities are included as well."

"Oh, not just living facilities, Meredith," said Joey. "I've taken the liberty of setting up a room for you on the South side of the building. It's a corner room, on the first floor, with windows all around so that you can have the best light, if you choose to use it for your studio. There's a sink, plenty of space, lots of storage, and room to talk to clients. Of course, it can be changed and redone any way you like."

"Joey, I told her that you said something about another place, too," said Nicholas.

Joey nodded. "I did. And the same opportunities will be there."

"Oh, Joey, we can talk to them about all of that later. Right now, let's get them some lunch," said Misty.

The group began walking toward the food area, and Joey explained. "Food is free in the cafeteria. If you don't see anything that you like in the prepared foods, just ask, and one of the cooks will be glad to whip up whatever you want." He leaned down to Karen and said, "They can even make your fast food favorites. Or something that you don't get very often."

Karen's eyes were wide. "Even pecan and blueberry pancakes? With maple syrup?"

Joey laughed. "Yes, honey, if that's what you want...and if your mom says it's okay."

Misty said, "We try to be a family here. First names are used often, and if you hear someone say 'mister' or 'miss', it isn't because we encourage it. They're either new, or they can't seem to adjust to the relaxed atmosphere."

They had reached the lunch line. One of the cafeteria workers, a young man wearing a chef's hat and a name tag that read "Butch" said, "Hi! What can I get for you folks today?"

Joey said, "Butch, give these people whatever they want. This is Nicholas Turner, and he's been offered our latest partnership. The lady and the little girls are his family."

Butch smiled. "I'll set them up right, Joey, don't you worry!"

"Misty and I will be over at the table. Please join us when you have your food," Joey said to Nicholas.

"We will," replied Nicholas.

Once the family had their trays, they joined the group at the table.

"So, uh, Nicky," said Snickers. "When were you going to introduce me to your, you know, daughter?"

Nicholas noted that "you know" had crept back into the man's remarks. Something had made him nervous.

"I meant to some time ago, Snick, but I just couldn't find the *right* time," said Nicholas. "Then, when today came and we needed your skills, we couldn't find you. Madeline said that something was trying to block her, to keep her from finding you. Then, when she did find you, the only way we had of getting you out of there quickly was for Madeline to do her stuff." He looked into his friend's eyes. "I'm sorry to spring it on you the way I did, but I didn't have a choice."

"It's okay, Nicky. At least, you know, I finally met her," said Snickers.

"Nicholas, Marcus has filled us in on most of Madeline's background, but the question that had been asked just before you came in was, 'What are Madeline's power bolts?' Can you tell us, Madeline?" asked Joey.

Madeline nodded as she chewed her bite of cheeseburger. "Sure. They're mostly energy, almost like 'lectricity, but they're made up of *good* energy. That's why they're white. Bad energy is the same thing, but it's black." She took another bite. "This is good, Karen! You were right!"

"Well, of *course! Duh!*" said Karen. "I know a *few* things, Madeline, gosh!" Karen grinned into her sandwich. "Winghead."

"Stinkbomb!"

"Featherbrain!"

"Monkeybutt!"

"That is enough, girls!" said Meredith sternly. But, she was too late, the girls had broken into giggles, as had most everyone sitting at the table.

"Madeline, do your power bolts hurt?" asked Misty.

Madeline nodded as she answered. "Yes, but only if you're bad. If you're good, they just pass right through you."

Misty smiled. "I see. Thank you."

Madeline smiled back. "You're welcome, Misty."

"Hey, Nicky, what did you, you know, need me for, anyway?" asked Snickers "I mean, you know, don't get me wrong or anything, you know, I'm glad you showed up when you did, you know?"

Nicholas replied, "It's about the kidnapping this morning."

"What kidnapping?"

Nicholas looked around the table. "You haven't told him?"

Marcus said, "No, we haven't had time."

Nicholas took a breath "Here's the deal, Snick..." Nicholas told him about the kidnapping of the children.

Snickers wrinkled his brow in thought. "I think I can, you know, help you out on this one. I talked to a guy-that-might-have-mentioned-a-guy type of thing, you know?"

"Can you find out?" asked Joey.

"Sure, you know? Just get me a phone and some, you know, privacy. I'll see what I can do," said the small, nervous man.

"I got this one, guys," said Dexter. "Mr. Thompson, would you like to come with me? I can get you whatever you need."

"Sure...Dexter, right?" replied Snickers "Hey, call me 'Snickers', you know?"

"Glad to, Snickers. You can call me Dex."

The two men walked out of the cafeteria.

As the remaining group chatted, Turk rose and said, "Got some work. Later." To Nicholas, he said, "Lemme know when you're ready to sign those papers. I gotta notarize them."

Nicholas nodded. "I will, Turk. Thank you."

No one was looking at Madeline.

The child-angel had dropped her cheeseburger onto her plate, and had a dazed look on her face. Her eyes were staring out at something far away, and at nothing at the same time.

Madeline was in a trance.

She was receiving instructions.

"You've actually prepared a studio for Meredith?" asked Nicholas.

Joey nodded. "We had an extra room on this floor, and it wasn't being used. There is an identical room in the plans on the second site, if you're interested in taking it on."

Megan said to Meredith, "Another thing to consider is that we have a staff physician. Access to Dr. Bishop is free to any member of the company."

Madeline's lips began to move, but no sound was coming out.

"Is he a good doctor?" asked Meredith.

"Oh, yes. Joey stole him from the FBI. He offered him more money and a top-notch clinic onsite. The clinic will be replicated at the second site, and the doctor will be there a couple of days a week, or as needed. Dr. Bishop is a good surgeon, too, isn't he, Megan?" said Misty.

"I thank God every day that he is," said Megan "When we first met up with Esteban Fernandez, one of the bullets his men fired up at my helicopter ricocheted and hit me in the shoulder. Dr. Bishop did such a good job on bringing me back to speed, that Joey hired him. Joey told the doc that he only wanted the best to work for Justice Security."

Madeline was now whispering.

"I can't hear you, winghead!" said Karen. "You have to talk louder!"

Everyone turned to Madeline.

"Oh, *shit,*" said Nicholas.

"What's wrong?" asked Joey.

Nicholas glanced at Joey, then he looked back at Madeline. "She's getting orders from her maker. All we can do is wait."

As Madeline whispered, a single tear ran down her cheek.

"Dear God, it must not be good news," said Nicholas. "I've never seen her cry during one of these trances."

"Oh, I hope it's not the children," said Jessica. "I pray that they're safe."

"Thechildrenaresafethechildrenaresafethechildrenaresafe,"   muttered Madeline. Suddenly, Madeline returned to herself. To Nicholas, she wasn't there, and then she was.

The little girl threw her head back, and at the top of her 'angel' voice, she opened her mouth and screamed, "*NOOOOOOOO!*" The sound came from everywhere at once, and was loud enough to shatter all of the glasses in the cafeteria, and all of the bulbs in the light fixtures. She was glowing with a bright blue light that hurt the group's eyes if they looked at her.

At the front desk, Tony Armstrong covered his ears with his hands, and still heard the voice clearly enough to hurt his head.

On the fourth floor, Turk had just settled down into his desk chair when the sound reached him. It wasn't loud enough to shatter the glass on the fourth floor, but it drove Turk immediately to his knees in prayer.

In the computer and IT room, everyone had to cover their ears, but the only casualty was a single water glass. It shattered just as the word was fading out. Dexter shared a look with Snickers and said with a calm voice, "That can't be good."

In the cafeteria, everyone had covered their ears and closed their eyes. The falling glass from the light fixtures didn't hit anyone, because, even in her anguish, Madeline had managed to throw protective energy shields over everyone in the room. The glass bounced harmlessly off of the invisible shields.

When the scream was done, the little girl sat crying deeply, with an earnest and heartfelt pain.

Chapter 8

No amount of persuasion could get Madeline to talk about her conversation with her maker.

"I'm not 'sposed to tell, Daddy," said Madeline, in between bouts of crying. "It's 'sposed to happen the way it happens. I'm not 'sposed to change it. And I can't tell any of you about any of it. I'm sorry, Daddy. Please don't be mad at me."

"Oh, honey, none of us are mad at you," said Nicholas "Everyone here understands that you have two fathers."

Madeline threw herself into her father's arms, and began crying passionately again.

Nicholas picked Madeline up, and turned to Joey. "Joey, can we go back upstairs now?"

"Of course. Meredith, if you would like a tour of the building, I can have Tony show you around," said Joey.

Meredith looked at Nicholas, who nodded. She took Karen's hand and said, "That would be very nice, Joey. Thank you."

As the group headed for the elevators, Joey stopped off at Tony Armstrong's station, the reception desk, with Meredith and Karen. "Tony, would you please show the Turner ladies around the building?"

"Of course, Joey, I'd be happy to. Just let me get someone up here to cover for me, and I'll take them right away," replied Tony.

"Thanks, Tony. Bring them to the situation room when the tour is done."

"Yes, sir."

Joey joined the group at the elevators just as the doors slid open. Everyone was silent on the ride up, with the exception of a few sobs from Madeline. The little girl clung to her father with a tight grip.

Turk couldn't take his eyes off of the little girl as the group went down the hall to the situation room.

Inside, Nicholas gently put Madeline down in one of the chairs. The pictures of the kidnapped children that Dexter had brought up were still on the monitors.

Nicholas studied the pictures for a moment, because there was something about them that was bothering him. Something he had forgotten.

Suddenly, he smacked his forehead with the palm of his hand, then said, "Marcus!"

Marcus had been going over something from his briefcase with Tory "What?"

"C'mere!" Nicholas knelt beside Madeline as Marcus and Tory came over. "Madeline, can you do something for me?"

Sniffling, Madeline replied, "What, Daddy?"

"Can you focus on the picture of one of those children and go to them? Like you went to Karen?"

"Of course, Daddy," said Madeline with exasperation. "Why didn't you ask sooner?" She pointed to a monitor that had a picture of a boy. "How about him?"

"That would be great, sweetpea," said Nicholas. "Don't forget to bring him back with you."

"You mean she could've rescued those kids an hour ago?" said Marcus.

Nicholas laughed. "Of course she could have!"

"So why didn't she?"

"We just didn't think to ask her!"

Madeline smiled at Marcus. "I'm only allowed to help when I'm asked to, Marcus."

Marcus looked at Joey. "I will be tee-totally damned."

"I'm still lost," interjected Tory. "What does this mean?"

"Madeline travels by thought, and she can make others travel by thought, too. You saw it earlier today when we rescued Snickers. She can concentrate on one of the kids, and go to that kid, no matter where that kid happens to be," said Nicholas.

"And bring him back?" asked Tory.

"And bring him back. Maybe a couple of others," answered Nicholas.

"Sounds like a plan to me," said Joey. "What do you need from us, Madeline?"

Madeline shook her head. "Nothing, Joey. All I have to do is cons-trate." To Nicholas, she said, "I'll be right back, Daddy."

"Be careful, sweetpea."

Madeline smiled, and then closed her eyes.

Nothing happened.

Madeline's eyebrows wrinkled in concentration.

And nothing happened.

Madeline took a deep breath and squeezed her eyes tight with concentration.

Still nothing happened.

Madeline's face smoothed out, then held a puzzled expression. She opened her eyes, and looked at Nicholas.

"Daddy, something's blocking me."

Everyone in the room was silent, and looked at each other.

Nicholas said, "What do you mean, sweetpea?"

"Something's blocking me. It's keeping me from finding that boy."

"Has that ever happened before now?" asked Joey.

Madeline shook her head. "It's never happened at all."

Nicholas looked at his daughter. "Try another kid."

"Okay, Daddy." She pointed to a little girl. "I'll try her this time."

Madeline closed her eyes. After a moment, she tilted her head with that same puzzled look on her face.

Madeline opened her eyes and looked at her father. She shook her head. "Nothing, Daddy. Not a glimmer. I'm being blocked from all of them."

"Who could block your power that way, sweetpea?" Nicholas dropped his voice a bit. "It's not God, is it?"

Madeline shook her head. "No, Daddy, although He could do it if he wanted to."

Nicholas looked puzzled. "Who else has the power to do that, Maddie?"

Madeline shrugged. "There are some angels that are more powerful than me, like the archangels, but why would an angel block me? Then, there are creatures working for the dark that could block me, too."

"Can you tell who's blocking you?"

"No, Daddy. I wish I could, but it's never happened before. I don't know what to look for."

"Hey, Madeline, not to change the subject or anything, but can I ask you something?" said Louie abruptly. "Somethin's been botherin' me since we were in the cafeteria."

"Sure, Louie, what is it?"

Frowning, Louie said, "Downstairs, you said you wasn't 'sposed' to tell us what your instructions are. Does that mean you *can't* tell us, or just that you aren't supposed to?"

Madeline abruptly looked down. "I'm not 'sposed to, and I'm not going to."

"Listen, little girl, is there anything you *can* tell us about all that?"

She looked up, first at Louie, then at Joey. "I can tell you that you're 'sposed to give Snickers a job in your computer security department, and you're 'sposed to pay him really good, 'cause he's worth it, and you'll need him. He's 'sposed to head up your second place's computer stuff."

Joey nodded. "You've got a deal, little one. I'll do it as soon as Dexter gets him back up here."

"Thank you," Madeline said timidly. "And I know what you're gonna offer to Daddy. He'll do it. So will Meredith."

Joey looked closely into Madeline's eyes. "What about you, Madeline? Will you go, too?"

The little girl looked away from Joey, and gazed at nothing. Very quietly, she said, "I don't know." A single tear ran down her cheek. "He won't tell me."

Chapter 9

D exter and Snickers burst into the situation room.

"Nicky!" Snickers was excited. "I got it!"

Everyone stood.

Nicholas said, "What, Snick?"

Snickers looked at the notepad that he was carrying. "The kidnappers! I found 'em! They're holed up in a warehouse on the corner of Fourth Street and Oak Avenue."

Marcus pointed his finger at Snickers as he spoke. "Hey, I know that place!" To the rest, he said, "It's that old abandoned steel-sided warehouse. You know the one! It's all rusty on the outside, with big windows."

Louie smiled. "I know just what you talkin' about, Marcus. I chased a gangbanger in there once. Lots of open space inside, but I don't know about any place in there to keep all them kids."

Joey frowned. "We'll have to assume that they're in there." To Marcus, he said, "Okay, Mr. In-Charge...what do you want to do?"

Marcus frowned. "Joey, I want you to take charge of this. Use as many of your people as you need. I'll come with you, and I'll keep the city cops off of you while you do what you do." He thought for a minute. Then, to Nicholas, he said, "Nicky, I want you and Madeline to go, too. Madeline might be able to 'poof' her way inside and see if the kids are in there."

Nicholas nodded. "Good enough, old friend. Let me tell Meredith, and we'll be ready."

Joey said, "I'll have Tony paged."

Nicholas shook his head. "No need, Joey. Madeline, take us to Meredith."

Joey said, "Hey, ask Meredith if you can sign the papers now."

"Will do. Madeline?"

"Okay, Daddy." Madeline took her daddy's hand, closed her eyes, and the two of them winked out of sight.

Louie said, "I ain't *never* gonna get used to that!"

Joey squeezed Louie's arm. "We're going to *have* to get used to it, old friend."

TONY WAS ON THE ELEVATOR with Meredith and Karen, explaining the differences between the guest quarters on the fifth floor and the apartments on the sixth floor, when Madeline and Nicholas winked into being with them.

"The apartments would probably be a better choice for you as a family because they...*Holy Shit!*" Tony prepared to draw his weapon, but Meredith touched his arm.

"It is only Nicholas and Madeline, Tony. Please do not be frightened."

Tony looked sheepish. "Sorry. They just took me by surprise."

The elevator dinged, and the doors opened onto the sixth floor.

As the group stepped out, Nicholas spoke. "Honey, Snickers found out where the kidnappers are hiding out. Marcus wants Madeline and me to go with them."

"Do I need to tell you to be careful?" asked Meredith.

Nicholas smiled. "No, my love. Oh, and Joey wants me to sign the papers before we go. Are we good to go on that?"

Meredith searched her husband's eyes. "Yes, Nicholas. Sign them. These people will be great friends, and a wonderful extended family."

Nicholas nodded. "I think so, too."

Meredith impulsively kissed Nicholas. "Please do be careful. I am frightened by this job. It makes me worry about both of you."

Nicholas smiled at his wife. "Piece of cake." To Madeline, he said, "Let's go."

They winked out of sight.

FATHER AND DAUGHTER winked back into the situation room. Everyone seemed to be in a rush. Joey was giving orders to everyone still in the room.

"Jim. I think it might be best if you loaded Tory up and left for Sardis County. First thing in the morning, okay? Have you heard from Patty or Brandon?"

Jim answered quickly. "Yes. Patty can meet us there whenever we go. Brandon still hasn't made up his mind."

Joey looked disappointed. "Crap. I hope he stays with us." To Tory, he said, "Tory, are you ready to hit the ground running?"

Tory nodded. "I am, subject to Chief Moore's orders."

"You have them," said Marcus. "Now, both of you get out of here. This could be sticky, and we don't want anything that's going to keep you here any longer than necessary."

As Jim Dandy and Tory Masterson turned to go, Joey called to them. "Jim, keep that building moving as quickly and as quietly as you can!"

Jim smiled his hundred-watt smile. "Be careful, Joey. Try not to blow anything up."

"No promises. Snickers!"

Snickers, who had been watching all of the activity with fascination, whipped his head around to look at Joey.

"Mr. Justice?"

"I need a top-notch computer person to head up the IT department at our new facility. You'll be in charge of setting it all up and maintaining it under the direction of Dexter. It pays top money, you'll have living facilities in the building, and you'll have free food available in the building's cafeteria twenty-four-seven. You'll be working with Jim Dandy. Want the job?"

Snickers, wide-eyed, said, "Sure! I need to, you know, give a little notice to my current, you know, job."

Joey nodded. "Welcome to Justice Security, Mr. Thompson. You're with us because I only want the best. Now, get with Dexter and work out when you can start training. I'll want you in on the ground floor of this, because you'll be building the IT department yourself."

Snickers looked at Nicholas. "Nicky! I've, you know, hit the big time!"

Nicholas laughed. He was overjoyed for his friend. "Snickers, I couldn't be happier for you!"

Joey interrupted. "Hold up. Nicholas. Are you ready to sign?"

Nicholas nodded.

So did Joey. "Good. Turk! Bring the partnership papers!" He turned to Snickers. "Don't go anywhere, Snickers. Not yet."

Turk brought the partnership papers to Nicholas.

Nicholas scanned them. *Is this up to speed, Madeline?*

*Yes, Daddy. You'll be making...*and she told him the figure.

Nicholas widened his eyes in awe. It was three times what he made on his own. Quickly, he scribbled his signature on the line that Turk had marked.

Turk smiled. He took out his notary stamp and imprinted the papers, then signed his name and the date alongside the imprint. He looked at Nicholas and held out his huge hand. Nicholas shook it.

"Welcome aboard, sir."

Joey watched as Turk nodded to him. "Welcome to Justice Security, partner." Joey shook hands with Nicholas. "Now, about that second facility. We really need a second partner on site. I would prefer that it be you. You aren't as widely visible as most of us, and you know Jim and Snickers. You're calm under pressure. And, it seems that you have a secret weapon that we didn't know about." He patted Madeline's head. "I'd like you and your family to help Jim with the building in Sardis County...if all of you agree, that is. Wouldn't want Meredith mad at me."

Nicholas was blown away. *Partnership in Justice Security, a new facility in Sardis County, living facilities, studios, offices, working with Snickers and Jim Dandy, and our own FBI man. I am blessed! I wonder if Meredith will move...I'd sure like to take the job there...Karen could go to school outside of this awful city! And so could Madeline, if it ever comes up...*

Meredith will move, Daddy. Madeline's voice was inside her daddy's head. *Her biggest worry will be what to do with the house.*

Nicholas laughed out loud, and hugged Madeline.

Joey, meanwhile, had given out radios to everyone. "Use encrypted channel seven, everyone!" Into his radio, Joey said, "Megan, are we ready to go with the artillery and the SWAT teams?"

The radio came to life. "Yes, we are, Joey."

Joey continued. "Misty, are the armored vehicles ready?"

"Ready when you are, honey."

"Doctor Bishop," Joey said into the radio. "Do you have everything you need for a mobile medical emergency unit?"

"Ready as we can be, Joey."

"Louie, radio equipment ready?"

"All set, Joe."

"Dexter, do you have plainclothes and uniformed personnel ready to go?"

"I do."

Jessica stood near Joey inside the situation room.

Joey said, "Jess, please stay here. I'd like you and Turk to coordinate for us from here."

"Got it, Joey. Ready, big man?"

Turk nodded.

"Then let's get it on!" said Jessica.

To Nicholas, Joey said, "The idea is that we're going to overwhelm the kidnappers with numbers. They won't have a lot of choice but to surrender."

Nicholas nodded. "I hope it works. If not, we have our secret weapon...right, Madeline?"

Madeline nodded half-heartedly. *Daddy doesn't understand what's going to happen, Father. May I please, please tell him?*

Silence answered her.

Madeline had never felt so frightened.

GARY MCGEE STUFFED half of his burger into his mouth.

McGee was a short man, five-two or so, with a flat nose. Some called him short to his face, but they only did it once. If he was short, so was his temper...and his fists were quick and accurate.

He looked around as he chewed. Juice from the tomato on his burger dribbled down his chin. McGee didn't notice.

The other two members of McGee's group sat around the card table with him, and each had a burger of their own.

Tim Wilson was a tall, rotund man with gray hair and a gray beard. He took large bites, and wiped his mouth fastidiously each time with cheap white napkins. He was not the brightest crayon in McGee's box, but he knew his explosives. He had set up the booby-trapped holding place with a cunning glee, knowing that the children would die no matter what, unless a deliberate sequence was followed. He had used enough C4 to leave nothing larger than an ear.

If Wilson was a bright blue in McGee's crayon box, Mike Bell was charcoal gray. Bell was an unintelligent man, often laughing at his own expense...never knowing that it was his own ignorance that he was laughing at. Fat, bearded, and dark-haired, Bell had two burgers, an order of French fries, an order of onion rings, and a half-gallon of diet cola. His method of eating was systematic: bite of burger, two fries, one onion ring, and a big gulp of soda...usually followed by a loud belch.

McGee swallowed, wiped his dripping mouth and chin, and said, "What tahm is it?"

Wilson took a look at the watch on his wrist. "One-thirty."

McGee slammed his hand onto the table. Bell jumped, then looked sideways at McGee to see if McGee was angry at him. He was not, so Bell resumed his steam shovel eating routine.

"Why ain't we heard anything yet? We left instructions for Justice as to what to do. He's supposed to call us. Why hasn't he? Doesn't he know those kids will die if he doesn't?"

Wilson swallowed his last bite. "Maybe he figures that you're gonna kill 'em anyway."

McGee looked at Wilson. "Ain't no way he'd think that."

Bell paused between bites. "You know, ah'm tard."

McGee snapped, "You're always tired. Shut up."

Wilson had his hand resting on his face, elbow resting on his other arm. "Yeah, I'm thinking he's thinkin' that we're gonna kill them kids anyway, and there's no point in giving himself up to us."

McGee looked at Wilson with disgust. "You sure have a pessimistic view of this situation. Either that, or you're tryin' to hoodoo me." He looked sideways at Wilson. "You didn't hook that stuff up to kill them kids, did you? I want them out if Justice follows the rules."

Wilson smiled. "No. I thought about it, but I didn't."

Bell said, "What are we gonna do with the rest of that C4?" He gestured with an onion ring toward a table heavily weighted down with the putty-like substance and several electronic triggers. Some were connected to C4, as if it was waiting to be used soon.

McGee said, "You can't remember nuthin', can you? We're gonna keep doin' this till we catch Justice. One way or another, we're gonna have him, and we're gonna collect that bounty."

Wilson said, "Just a thought, but what if Fernandez just kills us instead?"

"He won't."

"Are you sure?"

None of them noticed a brown-haired ten-year-old girl watching them. She faded from sight.

"As sure as I can be. But we'll be careful," said McGee.

Bell, a thoughtful look on his face, said, "Ya'll reckon we might be putting the cart before the horse? We don't even have Justice yet."

McGee raised his hand to give Bell a backhand slap. He never completed it.

The phone on the card table rang. The three men stared at it with surprise. The caller ID said "Joey Justice".

"I ONLY SAW THREE MEN. They were talking about killing the kids anyway, and turning you over to somebody named Fernandez."

Joey nodded. "Thanks, Madeline. They didn't see you, did they?"

Madeline looked surprised at the idea. "Of course not!"

"Good girl! Okay, everyone set up?"

Nicholas looked around at the people deployed around the warehouse. Five armored army-type vehicles were spread around, along with several armored, bulletproof cars that were often used in everyday assignments. Two hundred and fifty people, both plainclothes security and uniformed grunts, all held automatic weapons aimed at the warehouse, ready for anything.

Joey had told Nicholas about the tank, but he had decided not to use it. It made far too much noise for this kind of action.

"Looks like everyone is ready, Joey," replied Nicholas.

"I'm so glad we were able to ping this number and pinpoint the warehouse," observed Joey.

Into his encrypted radio, Joey said, "Okay, people. Showtime." He dialed the number that the kidnappers had given him.

THE PHONE ON THE TABLE rang for a third time.

Wilson said, "Phone won't answer itself, Gary."

McGee gave Wilson an angry look. He picked up the phone and said, "Hello, Justice. I was startin' to think that you were gonna let them kids die."

"Not likely, McGee."

"So, here's what I want you to do..."

"No, this is what *I* want *you* to do, McGee. I want all three of you to step outside of the warehouse and surrender. You're surrounded."

Gradually, as the words registered, McGee's eyes widened.

"Neat thing about snitches, McGee. They don't like people that hurt children."

McGee gestured to Wilson to look out a window.

"And technology is great, too. We used your number to pinpoint your location through cell towers."

Wilson had run from one window to a second one. He turned to McGee and made a twirling motion with his finger.

McGee's anger grew. His face turned red. "If you don't get those people away from here right now, Justice, you'll never know where those kids are!"

"Wanna bet, McGee? Why don't you trot out here and we'll talk about it. Come on. Be a good little Fernandez bitch."

McGee jumped to his feet, slammed the phone onto the concrete floor of the warehouse, and picked up a small Uzi.

"Grab your guns! We're going out fightin'!"

THE FIRST BURST OF automatic weapons fire came from the front window of the warehouse. No one was injured – everyone outside had cover.

Joey said into his radio, "Hold your fire! Hold your fire! Don't fire until I do! We have to take them alive! Repeat: We have to take them alive!"

Joey and Nicholas heard a burst of gunfire from the side of the warehouse.

Louie's voice came across the radio. "Dey shootin' at us, Joe! We're not shootin' back...yet."

"Hold on, old friend. If I can pinpoint one of them, I'll take him out. Maybe that will make the other two surrender."

"Heard dat, Joe."

Another burst of gunfire came from the front window. Joey happened to be looking as the muzzle flashes came from inside.

"Nicholas, I think I know where he is. Here, take my radio."

Joey handed his radio to Nicholas and raised his weapon. He carefully aimed to the right of the window. He fired a short burst, left to right, across the right wall on the side of the warehouse.

THE THIRD BULLET FROM Joey's burst traveled through the thin metal siding, barely missing a large wooden support post. It traveled on a straight course after that, and came to a halt inside an electronic trigger.

When the bullet hit the trigger, the trigger sent a small electric charge through its wiring.

The wires ended inside a block of C4 explosive. The charge was enough to set off the block of C4.

The block of C4, in turn, set off the remaining explosives on the table.

The warehouse blew outward with a huge explosion.

What was left of it caught fire, and burned merrily, sending a huge ball of fire and smoke into the air.

Everything...and everyone...inside the warehouse was vaporized.

JOEY WATCHED AS THE smoke and fireball floated into the sky...and, with it, his chances of finding the missing children from the school bus.

His radio crackled as Louie's voice came across.

"Joey? What the *fuck*, man? Did you *have* to blow this one up?"

Chapter 10

Two hours later, at three-thirty, the partners of Justice Security trudged into the situation room. Each one slumped into a chair, depressed and defeated. They had never felt this helpless on a case, even when Esteban Fernandez was at his worst.

Joey felt worse than all of them.

Everyone had reassured him. It wasn't his fault. No one had any idea that the C4 was inside the building, and Madeline hadn't noticed it, or she would have told them. Nicholas didn't understand why everyone was reassuring Joey, until Louie pulled him aside and told him about Joey's unfortunate reputation of making things explode completely by accident.

Marcus had taken over the scene and the investigation after the explosion. He made a couple of phone calls, and had the FBI crime lab people crawling all over the warehouse once the fire had been put out, looking for any type of clue that would tell them where to find the children. He had also kept the city police at bay by telling them that it was a Federal investigation, and any interference would not be tolerated.

Marcus then sent the Justice Security people away. A bit distracted, he said, "Look, if you guys can come up with something, I'm all ears. Otherwise, I'll just wait for the five o'clock explosion, and I'll pick up the pieces there."

Jessica looked at her friends and partners. Her heart weighed heavily, not only for the probable loss of the children, but the deep sorrow and defeat that her partners felt. If she had been able to take the burden away from them, she would have taken it in a heartbeat.

Madeline was staring at Jessica. She could feel the empathy that Jessica had for her partners, and she wished that she could do something to fix the pain inside Jessica. Her Father's words had been specific, however: *they must find their own way, and come to the decision on their own. Once they do, it will be up to you to see it through.*

Madeline had then asked, *Must it be that way, Father? Must I take them to that dangerous thing? I know that I can help them without a sacrifice on their part.*

And Madeline's answer to her question was...silence.

Madeline shared the partners' feelings of sorrow and defeat, but not for the same reason. Someone would be sacrificed today, maybe more than one, and she had no idea who that sacrifice would be...nor was she allowed to tell them that there had to be at least one. She knew that, if it was to be her daddy, she would happily sacrifice herself to give him more years in this lifetime.

Nicholas glanced around at his new partners. "There has to be something we can do! Somebody somewhere had to have seen those children!"

Misty replied. "True, Nicholas. But we only have an hour and a half. Even if we find them, we still have to have time to neutralize the explosives."

Megan said, "I have no doubt that Dexter could defuse whatever bomb is there, but we have to be able to find it before we can defuse it."

Louie looked up at Nicholas. "Think Snickers could track them down?"

"I'm sure that he could, but not in an hour and a half."

Louie shook his head, and looked at the floor again. "Of all times for Joey to send those guys to Hell! I wish he could've waited just a little while. Can't ask 'em *shit* where they are right now."

Everyone in the room sat quietly.

Joey kept running Louie's words through his head. *Joey sent 'em to Hell. Can't ask 'em* shit *where they are right now...Joey sent 'em to Hell...Can't ask 'em shit...can't ask 'em shit...sent 'em to Hell...*

"Why can't we ask them?" Joey said quietly. A thought was dancing on the edge of his mind.

"What did you say, Joey?" asked Dexter.

"I said, 'why can't we ask them'?"

Misty said very slowly, "Because they're *dead,* sweetheart."

"And hopefully roastin' on an open fire in Hell," added Louie. "And I hope it's their chestnuts that's roastin'!"

Joey shook his head. "I know that, Misty! But why *can't* we ask them?"

"Joey, what are you yabbering about?" said Jessica.

Instead of answering Jessica, Joey asked, "Nicholas, can Madeline take us to McGee? To Hell?"

Madeline's stomach dropped. Here was the thing that she had been waiting for, and dreading, just as her Father had told her. They had come to it by themselves.

The implication hit Nicholas like a punch to the solar plexus. "I...we...I don't know." To Madeline, he said, "Maddie? Can you take us there?"

Madeline stared at the floor. Her hair covered her face. She mumbled something.

"I'm sorry, sweetpea, I didn't hear you," said Nicholas.

Slightly louder, Madeline said, "Yes." Becoming suddenly animated and excited, she ran to Nicholas. "Daddy, please don't ask me to take you! Please! It's dangerous for everyone!"

Nicholas hugged his daughter. "Maddie, if there's the slightest chance that we can save those children, you know we have to go."

Between sobs, Madeline said, resigned, "Okay, Daddy. If we have to."

Nicholas took Madeline by the shoulders and looked into her face. "This is the big one, isn't it?"

Madeline nodded slowly.

"Sweetpea, there isn't a person in this room that wouldn't gladly go to their deaths if it meant saving those children."

"I know." Madeline sighed. "I just need to know what's going to happen."

Nicholas smiled at her. "Would it change things if you *did* know?"

Madeline shook her head and looked at the floor.

"Sometimes, sweetpea, not knowing is better." Nicholas reached for Madeline's chin and tilted it up. He looked into her eyes. "Do you understand why?"

Madeline shook her head. "No, Daddy. I don't."

Jessica said, "May I, Nicholas?"

Nicholas nodded.

"Madeline, if no one knows what's going to happen, then there's no built-in hesitation to do everything possible. If I knew that I was going to die by trying to save those children, then I might not do everything that I could do. I'd hold back, knowing that I was about to die."

Realization slowly dawned on Madeline's face.

"I see that you get it, munchkin," said Jessica. She gestured at the people in the situation room. "We all get that one or more of us may die doing this, if this is the thing you've been afraid of. But, if so, we go down fighting. Every last one of us."

"But I don't want any of you to die," said Madeline.

"Remember what I told you, sweetpea," said Nicholas. "I'd rather die doing good things than to grow old thinking I could have done more." He abruptly smiled. "Besides, if you don't know who's going to die...well, maybe the plan is that *nobody* dies. Had that occurred to you?"

Madeline's face reflected a glimmer of hope. She shook her head.

"So, you need to keep your hopes going, sweetpea."

"Okay, Daddy."

Joey spoke. "Madeline, I have to ask. Will you take us to Hell?"

Madeline nodded as she answered. "I will. I don't want to, Joey, but I'm 'sposed to."

TONY WAS STILL ESCORTING Meredith and Karen around. Joey had said to show them everything, and that's just what he was doing.

Dr. Bishop had requested the family's medical history in preparation. Meredith had filled out the required paperwork for the family...minus Madeline's, of course.

Dr. Caleb Mitchell, the in-house psychiatrist, had also spoken to Meredith, and assured her that he would be available for anything that she might need.

The cafeteria had requested a list of the family's favorite meals, in case Meredith...or Nicholas, for that matter...ever decided that cooking was more than they wanted to do on any particular night.

Tony had shown her the armory, the holding cells, the garage, and the automotive fleet, all of which were part of the underground stories of the Justice Security building. The computer/data processing/IT room was also underground, and Tony had given them the tour. He explained that the new facility would be identical to this one.

They were in the garage. Tony pointed out the tank.

"Want to go check that thing out, Karen?" asked Tony.

Karen's eyes widened. "Can I, Tony?"

"If it's okay with your mom."

Meredith showed concern. "Is there anything in there that can hurt her? Or us?"

Tony smiled. "No, ma'am. Not without the key. Only thing that will come on will be some lights."

Meredith took a deep breath. "Very well, Karen. You may. But be careful."

Karen ran to the tank and scampered to the opening. With a squeal of delight, she disappeared inside.

"This is wildly impressive, Tony."

"And you'll have access to all of it, Meredith. You're the spouse of a partner. We've never had one of those."

"None of the partners have been married?"

"There's Dexter and Megan, but Megan was a partner before they eloped. Joey and Misty are engaged, but they haven't set a date yet. And that's it."

"And who will be taking *your* job at the new facility?" asked Meredith.

"Her name is Lena Marrucci. She's in training right now. Lena used to be Jim's receptionist. Now, she's going to be lead grunt."

"And who will perform the job that Turk is doing?"

"Another Jim Dandy person. Her name is Emily Owens. She used to be Jim's executive assistant. She may go to Sardis County with Jim Dandy later."

"Are they capable, Tony?"

Tony actually stopped to reflect on Meredith's question. "I believe they are, Meredith. What they lack in experience they make up for with ability and enthusiasm."

"So Karen and I will be safe. Nicholas will have people to depend on that can help us."

"Yes, ma'am."

Meredith nodded. "I believe this will be a good thing, Tony, for all of us. Of course, this is assuming that everyone survives the day."

EVERYONE IN THE SITUATION room was talking at once.

Madeline said, "Hey! Everyone! I need to tell you some stuff!"

No one heard her, so she said it a bit louder.

Still no one paid any attention to her.

Angel-voice time, she thought.

"HEY!"

Everyone froze. Slowly, they turned to the little girl.

"Thank you. I have to tell you some stuff before we go," said Madeline. "It's important."

Nicholas, chagrined, said, "Go ahead, sweetpea. We're all listening."

"You've asked me to take you to the realm that you call 'Hell'. I've agreed to do it, but we will have to move quickly when we get there." Madeline began looking at each person as she spoke. "My presence there could be considered an act of war. 'Angels' are not supposed to appear there, and their 'demons' aren't supposed to appear in what you call 'Heaven'. We have to try hard to not get caught." She paused. "If we're caught, and a demon begins ringing the alarm bells – Hell's Bells – we will have to leave immediately. Should we get attacked by demons, I can die, if I'm hit by a strong dark power blast."

Joey's face paled. "Then maybe we shouldn't do this, Madeline."

Madeline looked into Joey's eyes. "Each of you is willing to die to save those children. So am I, Joey."

Louie asked, "Will those dark power blasts kill us, Madeline?"

"No, Louie. But it will hurt you like you've never been hurt before. I don't think we need to test that, okay?"

"You got it, little girl."

"You'll all be there as your regular human selves. You can't die there. But you can be hurt, and it can be for an eternity. A human caught there can be tortured, healed, and tortured again and again and again...just like the souls that we'll be looking for. Be careful, all of you."

"Will weapons work against them, Madeline?" asked Megan. "Like guns, or explosives?"

Madeline smiled. "They will if I bless them. By blessing them, I confer white power to them. It might not kill them, but it will sure hurt them a lot!" Her smile became broader. "The demons won't know what hit them."

Dexter was shaking his head.

"Is something wrong, Dexter?" asked Joey.

Dexter half-smiled. "I'm sorry. I'm still wrapping my mind around this whole angel-demon thing."

Nicholas spoke up. "I understand. It's a lot to take in in such a short period of time."

"Madeline," said Joey. "We're pressed for time. How soon can we get this done?"

Madeline took a deep breath. "I'm ready anytime, Joey."

"I'm not," said Nicholas. "Madeline and I need to talk to Meredith and Karen before we do this."

Wordlessly, Joey handed his radio to Nicholas.

Slightly surprised, Nicholas pressed the "send" button. "Tony, this is Nicholas Turner. Would you please bring my ladies to the situation room?"

Tony answered right away. "On our way, sir."

IN HIS PRIVATE OFFICE, or what would have been his private office if he and Meredith hadn't agreed to the Sardis County move, Meredith was shaken.

"Nicholas, you simply are *not* taking this risk with your life, *or* risking the life of your daughter with this lunacy!"

Nicholas put his hands on Meredith's shoulders and gently pulled her into his arms. As he hugged her, he quietly spoke to her.

"Meredith, there really isn't another way to save those children. I wouldn't even try it if there was. But, Madeline's ready to go, our new partners are ready to go...and so am I." He moved Meredith away from him so that he could look into her eyes. "Suppose I had stopped looking into Karen's disappearance just because it was dangerous...we never would have found her."

"I...I know, Nicholas. But...Hell? *Really?*"

Nicholas nodded. "Yes, really. If you believe in one, it's logical to believe in the other."

Fire appeared in Meredith's eyes. "Just make sure that you come back in one piece, Nicholas Turner. And bring our daughter with you!"

IN THE OPPOSITE CORNER of the room, Karen and Madeline were talking quietly.

"Madeline, do you have to do this?"

Madeline nodded. "Yeah."

"That sucks."

"Yeah."

Karen snuck a look at her adoptive sister. "Are you scared?"

Madeline nodded.

"Want me to come with, Winghead?"

Madeline's face showed fear. "No! It's too dangerous, Karen!"

"Then why are you going?"

Madeline lowered her head. "'Cause I have to."

"God?"

"Yeah."

The girls were silent for a moment.

"Will you be okay, Madeline?"

"I don't know, Karen. He won't show me."

More silence.

"I love you, Madeline."

"I love you, too."

Karen hugged her new sister.

"You better come back, Winghead. I don't care *what* God says."

THE TURNER FAMILY TRUDGED back into the situation room. Every head turned to look at them.

Nicholas took a deep breath. "We're ready."

Madeline looked around. "Someone needs to stay behind. This is the person I can focus on for the return. Meredith won't do, because we may need fast action when we come back, in case someone gets hurt."

Tony stepped up. "Madeline, I'll stay behind with your sister and your mother. You focus on me, and you'll get anything you need when you return."

Madeline looked into Tony's eyes. With a slight smile, she said, "Tony Armstrong. You did what you had to do. Stop blaming yourself." Her smile widened. "And thank you for being my home base."

The little girl turned to the rest of the people in the room. "Does anybody have any last questions?"

Not one person said anything.

"Okay. Time passes differently there. What seems like hours there will only be a minute or two here. To put that into something we can all understand, to Gary McGee, it's already been an eternity."

Everyone was still silent.

Madeline spread her hands. "So. Do we have weapons to bless?"

Chapter 11

The group stood in an uneven circle inside the situation room.
Madeline gave the group some final instructions.

"Try not to draw attention to yourselves. It's better if we can sneak in and out without being seen. As we travel, you can leave your eyes open or closed. It's up to you. Daddy, you and Joey will need to hurry to McGee and find out what you need to know. You can't threaten torture. He already has that. Offer him relief from torture. Offer him grace from me so that he enters Limbo. It's not Heaven, but it's better than Hell. Above all, have sympathy. Sometimes all it takes is one bad choice to wind up where he is.

"If we do have to fight, use your weapons sparingly. Fight hand-to-hand as needed. The noise from the weapons will draw more demons to the fight. And, if there's a fight, they will try to get you away from the others, so gather close around me as soon as you can get to me. Now, this is important, so pay attention. *If someone is separated and gets carried away by the enemy, none of you can follow.* It's a divide and conquer thing, so consider that person lost from us. It sounds mean, I know, but that's how it has to be. If you go after the separated person, you will get captured, too...and it will weaken the rest of us, and may cause all of us to be lost."

Madeline looked around at the circle of adult faces. "I don't know what my Father has planned for this trip. I don't know if all of us will survive...or if *any* of us will survive. I only know that it's His wish that we go. The choice to go belongs to each of you. Search your hearts, and be sure that it's what you want to do...and not what you feel that you must. If anyone wants to back out, say so. If you want to go, please hold hands."

Without hesitation, Nicholas reached out and took Madeline's hand. He looked into his daughter's eyes and smiled.

Joey took Madeline's other hand. He nodded once.

Misty took Joey's hand. "Where you go, my love, I go."

Percival "King Louie" Washington took Misty's hand. "Can't let my friends down. Or them kids. Let's go."

Dexter and Megan shared a look. Megan took Dexter's hand in one of her own, then took Louie's hand in the other. "We're in."

Dexter said lightly, "I always wanted us to travel to unusual places."

Jessica Queen looked around at her friends and co-workers. She looked at Meredith and Karen, sitting quietly at the situation room table with Tony Armstrong. She thought to herself, *I'll miss this the most, I think...gathering around the table and knowing we'll be fine, as long as we have each other.* To the others, she said, "Oh, *bollocks!* In for a penny, in for a pound, I suppose!" And she took Dexter's hand, and then she took Nicholas's hand.

The circle was complete.

Madeline once again surveyed her fellow travelers. "I'm sorry that our weapons are limited to what you can strap to yourselves, or carry inside your pockets or bags. But, we have to be touching to travel. Again, I'm sorry."

Nicholas squeezed Madeline's hand.

Madeline took a deep breath. "Okay, here we go!" She closed her eyes.

OH, MY...I NEVER KNEW anything could be so beautiful! thought Dexter. *Colors are so intense! And look at the orbs, going up and down!*

Almost before Dexter could complete the thought, he felt a rushing back to reality, and a light, jarring thud.

The journey was complete. Justice Security had gone to Hell.

Dexter looked around, and noticed that everyone else was doing the same thing...with one exception.

Madeline, appearing in her "angel" form, was not looking around. She was looking at the ground.

With awe, Dexter blurted, "Wow, Madeline! You're beautiful!"

And, with that observation, everyone else turned to Madeline. Jessica gasped.

Madeline raised her eyes to Dexter. "Thank you, Dexter." Her eyes were glowing a bright, clean blue. The power flows that draped down from each shoulder to form her "wings" were glowing a powerful, searing white. In this form, Madeline was slightly taller than her earthly self.

Louie noticed this. "You're taller, little girl."

A slight smile danced around the edges of Madeline's mouth. "In this form, in this place, I am more than Madeline. My angel form takes over here...one of the rules of my Father. In this place, I cannot hide who I am."

Joey spoke. "There's no light, but I can see."

Madeline nodded. "It's a black non-light. I know it doesn't make sense to you, but it works."

"Madeline, this place looks like a standard earth cave," said Nicholas.

"It is shaped by your mind into something you can comprehend. It's nothing like a cave, Daddy."

"Are we speaking, Poppet, or are we only thinking?" asked Jessica.

"We are speaking. But be sure to hold your voices down. We don't want to draw attention to ourselves," replied Madeline.

"How long we got here, little girl?" asked Louie.

Concern crossed Madeline's face. "Not as long as I'd like. Daddy, you and Joey need to go talk to Gary McGee...he's about two hundred feet in that direction." She pointed.

Nicholas nodded.

Joey said, "Okay, let's go, Nicky. Louie, will all of you please set up a protective perimeter circle around Madeline?"

Louie looked surprised. "Why, Joe? She de most powerful of all of us!"

Joey nodded. "She is. But she's also our only ticket back home. She has to be protected."

"Oh, shit! Man, I *never* thought of that!"

Worried looks crossed everyone's faces.

Misty leaned over and kissed Joey. "You hurry along, lover. We still have a wedding to plan."

"Yeah, Joey, hurry up," added Dexter. "I really don't want to see demons. An angel a day is enough, okay?"

Madeline stood in front of Joey. "Offer him my grace, Joey. I can make that happen as soon as he tells you where the children are being held."

"Yeah, and be sympathetic," added Megan. "His problem could be ours with just one turn down the wrong path."

Nicholas smiled, and took his daughter's hand. "Don't worry, sweetpea. I'll keep Joey straight. You watch out for these guys, okay?"

Madeline smiled, but there was a slight strain in it. "I will, Daddy. But, I'm very worried. Please hurry."

Nicholas smiled, trying to give his daughter faith. "On our way."

The two men began walking in the direction that Madeline had indicated.

Louie, Megan, Dexter, Misty, and Jessica surrounded Madeline protectively.

"WELL, NICKY, DID YOU ever in your wildest dreams expect to be in Hell?" asked Joey.

Nicholas chuckled. "Before I met Meredith, and before Madeline came to me, the last few years have felt like Hell. But, no, I never expected to literally *be* in Hell. Not this way, anyhow."

Joey sighed. "I almost wish I hadn't thought of this plan."

"You had to."

"Why?"

"If I have to tell you, you really are lost, Joey."

Joey smiled. "I know. The children. And I'm the reason that we're here, too."

Nicholas looked thoughtful. "Joey...have you ever thought that...well, that the 'accidental' explosions aren't really accidents?"

Joey looked surprised. "What? That I do it on purpose?"

Nicholas shook his head. "No. That the accidents are driven by...*other* considerations...*otherworldly* purposes."

Joey thought for a moment. "Well...I have to admit, almost every time it's happened, something good came out of it."

The two men walked a few steps.

Nicholas said quietly, "Since Madeline decided to share my life, I've learned that almost everything happens for a reason. And that it's all part of a plan that I'm not privy to."

"Maybe so. But I'd sure like to know how Fernandez fits into these...*plans*."

Nicholas stopped. He could hear faint moaning. "Do you hear that, Joey?"

Joey nodded. "It's coming from the other side of those boulders."

"MADELINE?" ASKED MEGAN. Her eyes continued scanning the surrounding area.

"Yes, Megan."

"How would they find out that we're here?"

Madeline took a deep breath. "Anything, actually. We could be overheard, or there could be a mystical boundary around Gary McGee, although it isn't likely. A resident could just happen to pass through here, and see us."

"So, pretty much anything that moves is an enemy, right?" asked Megan, adjusting the strap of the machine pistol over her shoulder.

Madeline smiled nervously, then nodded. "Yes."

GARY MCGEE COULDN'T remember a time that he wasn't in agony.

Ever since he arrived in this place, McGee's agony was repeated again and again. He was chained spread-eagled and naked to the rocks around him. The restraints around his wrists and ankles were so tight that they hurt constantly. He felt as if his circulation had been cut off in his extremities. His hands and feet tingled constantly. But, that wasn't the worst.

The worst was when the little monsters came.

At first, McGee thought it was going to be the end of him. The little monsters came sneaking over the boulders, three of them, each snapping their three-inch-wide mouths open and shut. Each mouth was full of tiny, razor-sharp teeth. The monsters looked like a cross between small iguanas and Chihuahuas. McGee had yelled at them, hoping that it would scare them off.

It didn't.

He had yelled for help.

None came. He had been utterly alone.

Yelling did no good.

When the first monster bit down on his exposed scrotum, McGee had screamed.

The second and third monsters also began feasting on McGee's exposed organs. McGee had never know such pain. The monsters kept tunneling their way into his lower body, eating his intestines, his colon, and his anus...all before starting on his kidneys and his stomach. When he looked down, McGee was covered in blood from his waist down.

McGee screamed until his voice was hoarse, and could make no sound. Mercifully, he passed out from the pain.

Later, when he woke up, McGee was still chained to the boulders.

He was whole again.

McGee couldn't believe it. He began laughing wildly, believing that he had perhaps dreamed the monsters.

Until the first one poked its head above a boulder...quickly followed by the other two.

McGee began to scream. He screamed through the pain. He screamed until he was hoarse, and his throat felt as if it were on fire.

He passed out a second time.

The third time, McGee woke up, saw that he was still chained, and began whimpering. He knew what was coming, even before the first monster's head popped into view.

Over and over, more times than he could count, McGee had gone through this hideous punishment. He finally figured out that he was in Hell, but he had no idea how he had gotten here. There had been no judgement, no pearly gates, no angels pointing accusing fingers.

McGee had just...shown up here.

He vaguely remembered exchanging gunshots with someone before he was here, but it was not sharp.

Then, he remembered the children. The busload of children he had booby-trapped, to try to get Joey Justice to give himself up. Yeah, give himself up so that...

McGee couldn't remember.

The children.

That had to be why he was here.

The children must have died, and McGee must have wound up here to pay the ultimate price for what he did to them.

Oh, God, if I could only undo what I did! I would accept Your punishment, but I shouldn't have done that to them kids!

The first monster had popped into view, and McGee's thoughts scattered.

JOEY AND NICHOLAS SAW the first monster take its first bite of Gary McGee's balls.

Both men were incredulous, and immediately went into action. They picked up fist-sized rocks and began hurling them at the monsters.

Nicholas scored first. His rock hit the first monster hard...so hard that it let out an ugly squawk. The other two turned toward the two men, and immediately scampered away over the boulders.

The first monster decided to fight. It faced the two men and bared its tiny sharp teeth. Joey pegged a rock at it that hit the side of its head. Nicholas followed with another rock that struck the monster's back leg hard enough to cause another ugly, unrecognizable squawk. The monster limped away from McGee, but stopped at the top of a boulder to look back at Nicholas and Joey. It seemed to be marking them in some way. Then, it disappeared into the boulders.

As Joey hurried over to McGee, Nicholas closed his eyes for a moment.

Madeline, baby, do you see these monsters in my mind? I think they have...

...GONE TO TELL ON YOU. Yes, Daddy, we're in trouble now. Hurry.

"Madeline? What's wrong, Poppet?" asked Jessica.

Madeline looked around the cavern and took a deep breath. "Daddy and Joey have just chased away some lesser demons. It's very likely that they'll tell what they know. We could be in big trouble now."

Megan said, "Weapons check. Everyone. Now."

"TONY? DO YOU THINK that they are okay?" asked Meredith.

Tony straightened his duty belt, and looked directly into Meredith's eyes.

"Meredith, Joey has looked into Esteban Fernandez's eyes and broken that demon-on-earth's nose. I think they're fine."

I hope, he didn't add.

"OKAY, I'LL ANSWER A few questions," said Marcus Moore, as he faced a group of reporters.

The reporters were behind barricades that had been set up by the city police on the scene, at the direction of the FBI.

Miriam Apple had arrived on the scene of the explosion with Steve, her cameraman and lover, in tow, as usual.

"Come on, Studley," said Miriam, as she had opened the van door.

They got out of the van. Steve stopped and stared at the explosion site. Miriam saw Steve staring, and looked at it herself.

"Wow!" she said to Steve. "I think that has Joey all over it, don't you?"

Steve smirked and nodded.

Miriam nudged Steve. "Come on, let's go see what we can find out."

They made their way to the group of reporters. They had just missed the announcement by Marcus.

"...anything to do with the kidnapping of the children this morning, Chief Moore?"

Marcus thought for a moment. "Yes. We had intelligence that led us to the suspects. They were hiding inside the warehouse that previously stood at this address. A gunfight broke out, and some explosives belonging to the suspects were triggered. There were no survivors."

Reporter voices clamored all around Marcus.

Miriam, shaken, called out. "Chief Moore, were the children here?"

The reporters fell silent.

Marcus saw that Miriam had asked the question. "No, Ms. Apple, they were not."

Relief flooded through Miriam, although she had no idea why her sudden hard-ass persona should be pierced.

The Channel Four reporter shouted, "Are there any surviving suspects, sir?"

Marcus took a deep breath before he answered. "No."

"Do you have any idea where the children might be?"

"Again, I have to say no. I would hope that anyone that might have any information would come forward now. We have a tight deadline, and any help we can get is welcome."

Channel Fifty-Eight's reporter spoke up. "Chief Moore, certain members of the city's police department have floated the idea that Joey Justice is more of a menace than a help to the safety of our city. Does the FBI agree?"

"No comment." Marcus stopped. "No, I'll answer that. Let me remind the citizens of this city that it wasn't too long ago that Joey Justice saved over thirty thousand people from being killed by Esteban Fernandez. I believe that the help far outweighs the menace. Anyone that feels differently is more than welcome to take it up with Esteban Fernandez...on their own, of course." He turned away from the crowd of reporters as they barked more incoherent questions. "No more questions."

"MCGEE?"

Joey had eased closer to the tortured soul. When Joey said the man's name, the man looked at him.

"*Justice?* In *Hell?* This must be some kind of new torment!" Tears came from his eyes. "Lord, I'm so sorry for the things I've done! Please show me some mercy."

Joey said, "McGee, it's really me. I'm here. I came to see you."

McGee looked at Joey. "Here? *Here?* How?"

Joey nodded his head at Nicholas. "His daughter brought us here. She's an angel, McGee."

"An angel?"

Joey and Nicholas both nodded.

Joey answered the man. "Yep. A full-fledged angel on earth."

"Why would you come here looking for me?"

"The children, McGee." Joey leaned closer. "When you died, you took their secret with you. We came to ask you where they are, and how they are booby-trapped. We want to save them."

Nicholas added, "All we can offer you in exchange is my daughter's grace. Madeline's grace will place you in Limbo for eternity...but it won't be torture, like here."

McGee was staring at Joey's face. "Justice, tell me this: how did I die?"

Joey frowned, and looked down. He lifted his eyes, and met McGee's. "It was an accident. One of my bullets hit some C-4 that you had inside the warehouse."

Tears shone in McGee's eyes. "Don't blame yourself, Justice. I had it coming." McGee sniffed. He turned to Nicholas. "I'll tell you both what to do to save the children, and I'll take your daughter's grace, sir."

Nicholas stared unseeing for a moment.

McGee looked concerned. "Justice! Is he okay?"

Joey smiled. "He's fine. He and his daughter communicate telepathically. He zones out when he's talking to her, but I don't think he knows it."

Nicholas focused on Joey. Fear was in his eyes. "Madeline said two things, Joey. The first one is that there are no accidents."

Joey looked surprised.

A loud, repeated gong sound began echoing through the cavern.

"And the second thing she said is that we have to hurry. They're under attack."

Chapter 12

The attack, when it came, began innocently enough.

A man-sized demon appeared, walking behind one of the small demons that had been tormenting McGee. Every couple of steps, the man-sized demon leveled a hard kick on the small demons backside. Neither demon showed any surprise, pain, or emotion about the casual violence. It appeared that they accepted it as a normal part of their existence.

Dexter saw them first. He reached out to Louie on one side, and to Megan on the other.

Madeline's voice came to the group, but it came from *inside* their heads. "Everyone freeze. Maybe they won't notice us."

Kick.

The smaller demon rolled along the floor of the cavern. It came to a stop directly in front of Louie. The demon stared at Louie, as if it didn't believe what it saw. Then, it shrieked.

The shriek startled the larger demon, and seemed to enrage him. He bore down on the smaller demon to inflict more violence, but it stopped when it noticed that the smaller demon was staring at Louie. It turned its gaze to Louie.

It was ugly. *Butt ugly,* thought Louie. *Damn! That must be a requirement for demons!*

Dexter whispered. "Louie, we gotta take it out."

Louie wasted no time. He drew a long knife from a sheath hanging from his belt, jumping at the demon at the same time.

The demon roared, and tried to raise its arms to block Louie. Louie was on it before it could block him, however. Dexter moved in and delivered a spinning kick to the side of its head, and it lost consciousness. It slumped to the ground.

Dexter was breathing hard. He and Louie stood side by side, looking down at the demon.

"You know we need to finish it, don't you?" said Dexter.

"I know," replied Louie.

Neither man moved.

"I can't do it, Louie."

"Me, either. It don't seem right."

Megan pushed past the two men, knelt down, and stabbed the demon through the heart. She stood, wiping her blade on her jeans. "Had to be done, boys." She looked around. "Where's the little one?"

The two men looked around, but the smaller demon was nowhere in sight.

"Oh, shit," said Louie conversationally.

"Hey, Madeline, the little one's gone!" called Dexter.

A look of fear crossed Madeline's face, but only Jessica noticed it. "Everyone get ready, because..."

Madeline was interrupted by a loud, repeating gonging sound.

"They're ringing! Hell's Bells are ringing! We're about to be attacked!" Madeline stopped long enough to telepathically talk to Nicholas and tell him about the attack.

Louie, Dexter, and Megan retreated back into the protective circle that they had formed around Madeline. Misty and Jessica completed the circle. All of the Justice Security people were facing away from Madeline. The circle meant that they could see danger from all sides.

They began talking, nothing more than a constant patter of nonsense. By using this method, they could keep up with each other as they faced the oncoming threat. If one person dropped out of the conversation, then the rest knew that the silent person had fallen, and that they needed to tighten the protective circle.

Demons began appearing from all over the cavern...all sorts of demons. Each demon was the stuff of nightmares. Some had tentacles, some had teeth that would make a great white shark envious, some had quills that dripped poison, and some defied description.

"I count at least three, four dozen!" shouted Misty.

"Me, too!" echoed Louie.

Madeline began glowing with a blinding white light that made several demons scream with anger and surprise. Her power began cascading from her shoulders at a faster rate, and her eyes glowed a deep, bright blue.

"FIGHT! FIGHT WITH ALL YOUR STRENGTH!" shouted Madeline in her strongest angel voice.

Some of the demons paused in their advance at hearing the angel's voice, not knowing if they should continue. They seemed confused. Others continued running directly toward the group.

Dexter had drawn a sword from a sheath that hung by his side, and stood ready to fight. Megan aimed her machine pistol at the advancing horde, as did Jessica and Misty. Louie took up a boxing stance, fists at the ready. Each weapon, including Louie's fists, glowed with a subtle white light from the blessing that Madeline had given them all before they departed.

Madeline fired first. A blast of pure white light shot from her hand and struck an advancing demon directly in its chest. The demon screamed, but the scream was cut off as the demon exploded.

Megan followed suit, firing her machine pistol at an advancing group. The white, glowing bullets cut down their opponents as they ran. Demons fell in a pile several feet in front of Megan, as she quickly reloaded her weapon.

Jessica and Misty began judiciously firing, choosing to fire two to three bullets at each demon, in an attempt to save their ammunition. Each shot fired from the two women dropped a demon.

Louie hit a demon on the side of its head, and it dropped like a stone. He hit another, and it dropped. Louie felt like he was in a free-for-all boxing match, and the opponents just kept coming.

Dexter had drawn a shorter blade from another sheath, and whirled like a deadly top. The two swords beheaded and maimed demons on all sides.

Madeline was firing white energy blasts from each hand, and demons exploded each time a blast connected.

Finally, the demons were all down.

Breathing heavily, Louie asked, "Are we done? Is that it?"

They all watched as the first demon, blown to bits by Madeline's white energy blast, reassembled itself as if by magic. It stood tall, looked at the group, and roared its defiance.

"NO!" answered Madeline.

The gong-like bells continued their echoing pealing. As the group prepared for battle again, many more demons began running toward them. The new demons were as varied as the imagination would allow, and some of the new arrivals had wings. Some were so tall that they had to stoop so as not to hit their heads on the ceiling of the cavern.

Suddenly, a huge black bolt of energy landed inside the group's circle.

Madeline's head circled around until she spotted the demon that had thrown the black bolt. It was standing on an elevated rock several feet away from them. It had pointed bat wings, and ram's horns emerging from its head. Its feet were cloven hooves, and its eyes were glowing with a dark red shine. It was grinning widely, showing a mouth full of sharp teeth.

As Madeline's brow furrowed, another demon, much like the first, appeared. It stood beside the first. Both demons threw black bolts of energy at Madeline. Madeline countered by firing her own white bolts at the demons. One of her bolts hit its target, and the demon blew to bits.

Two more appeared, bringing the total to three.

"Madeline!" shouted Jessica. "We're running out of ammunition!"

"USE KNIVES, SWORDS, AND FISTS! WE MUST HOLD THEM UNTIL DADDY RETURNS!"

Louie snuck a look over his shoulder at the angel. He was awed by her appearance. *She look like a force of nature right now! She beautiful, but deadly as can be! And I cain't help but love her!*

A KNOCK SOUNDED ON the door of the situation room.

Tony crossed to the door and opened it. Turk stood on the other side, with Marcus Moore beside him.

"Hi, Tony," said Marcus as he walked through the door. "I wanted to ask Joey..." He stopped talking as he noticed that no one was in the room but Meredith and Karen. "Meredith. Karen." He looked around, half expecting everyone to jump out and yell, "Surprise!" But no one did.

Marcus looked at Meredith again. "Meredith, where is everybody?"

"Marcus, they have all gone to Hell."

Thinking it was a joke, Marcus said, "How? In a handbasket?"

When Meredith didn't smile, Marcus looked closer. What he saw frightened him.

"You're serious, aren't you?"

Meredith nodded. "Madeline took them. They have gone to ask McGee where the children can be found."

Marcus looked at Tony, then at Turk. He saw the truth in their eyes. He slowly collapsed into a chair at the round table. "Oh, my God. Surely they know better than to go to Hell." He looked at Meredith. "Do they know how dangerous that might be for Madeline?"

Meredith nodded.

Marcus shook his head in disbelief.

"You must not blame Joey or Nicholas. Madeline took them all with no complaint, and of her own free will. Rescuing the children was paramount in her decision."

Karen said, "Yeah, Marcus. You gotta have faith in my winghead sister. She can *do* this!"

"LOUIE! MEGAN! I CAN'T DO THIS MUCH LONGER!"

Madeline was throwing white energy bolts as fast as she could. Each time she hit one of the grinning demons with the bat wings, two more appeared. Black bolts were flying all around the group. It was a miracle that no one had been hit by one.

The group was fighting, and fighting hard. Demons were falling all around, but most were regenerating. The group was getting tired, however. It would be long until the Justice Security people were outnumbered and overpowered.

Madeline threw her arms out to each side. Concentrating, the angel threw a white dome of energy around the group. Demons that hit the outside bounced off, and black energy bolts dissipated when they hit the dome.

"I CAN ONLY HOLD IT FOR A FEW MINUTES. REST. YOU WILL NEED IT."

Madeline spoke to Nicholas.

"...AND THAT'S HOW YOU disable the booby traps."

Joey nodded at McGee. "Easy enough. Thanks, McGee."

McGee looked at Joey. "I would have told you even if you hadn't promised the angel's grace. I wish I had never kidnapped them in the first place. If I'd known then what I know now, it never would have happened."

"McGee, it is what it is. We'll keep our word, too. Won't we, Nicholas?"

Joey turned to Nicholas. When he saw the man's face, Joey said, "What?"

Nicholas barely heard Joey over the bells. "Madeline says that they're out of ammunition, the group is spent, and Madeline can't hold all of the demons. We have to go. Now."

The two men stood. Nicholas looked at McGee. "McGee, my daughter tells me that she can't spend the energy right now to move you to Limbo, but that she will take care of you as soon as we get away. Can you forgive her?"

McGee nodded. "I believe you, and I believe her. Now, go save them, and don't worry about me."

Joey said, "Thank you, McGee."

The two men hurried back the way they had come.

THE FIVE PEOPLE LOOKED through the transparent dome of white light. Outside, demons pounded on the dome, and made all sorts of threatening gestures toward the group inside. The grinning demons with the bat wings fired black bolt after black bolt at the wall of the dome.

Louie noticed that with each time a black bolt struck the dome, Madeline winced.

I guess even angels get tired after a while. Lord, if you're listening, we could sure use a break here.

"Madeline, we're rested, honey," said Misty. "If you want to let it go, let it go. We'll fight, and we'll keep them off of you."

Madeline smiled a tortured smile. Her voice had returned to normal volume. "Thank you, Misty, but I can't let go. We're badly outnumbered here, and we'd be killed in nothing flat. Daddy and Joey are on their way back." Madeline winced as more black bolts hit the dome. "I just have to hold on until...*UNNNGGGHHH!*"

A huge black bolt had struck the outside of Madeline's protective dome, and it proved to be too much for her. The dome dissipated, and Madeline collapsed to her knees.

The demons appeared as surprised as the group of people. The surprise didn't last long, however. With a loud roar, the demons renewed their attack.

Louie began throwing punches again. *We are soooo fucked,* he thought to himself.

"Let me *GO*, dammit!"

Everyone turned to see what was going on.

The tall demon that walked with a stoop had grabbed Megan and tossed her over its shoulder. It was walking quickly away as Megan slapped and punched anywhere she could reach. They were almost out of sight.

Louie looked at Dexter. Dexter's face was incredulous. Louie's mind whirled. *I got to stop him, or we gonna lose 'em both!*

Louie threw his arms around Dexter just as he was preparing to take off after Megan and the demon. Dexter had taught Louie very well in the skills of martial arts, and Louie was able to counter anything that Dexter tried...and Dexter tried everything he could think of to break himself loose. Louie held firm.

"Let me go, Louie! They've got her, dammit!"

"Naw, man, I can't do it! I gotta keep you! I can't lose you both, man!"

"I can save her!"

"Naw, you can getcher self killed is what you can do! Ease up, Dexter!"

Just before the demon disappeared out of sight with Megan, Madeline leaned forward to throw a white power blast after it. If she hadn't leaned forward, the black power bolt that grazed her back and head would have hit her full-on. The graze still hit her hard, and she was blown into a pile. Her color faded. Her power cascades dribbled to nothing. She didn't move.

"Madeline!"

Nicholas and Joey had come into sight just in time to witness all of this. Both men began firing their machine pistols into the demons, scoring hits with every shot. Nicholas had a look of deep hatred on his face, while Joey's face reflected determination.

The two men soon made a path to their friends.

Nicholas ran to Madeline. He cradled her in his lap. When he looked up at Joey, tears were running from his eyes. "She's not breathing, Joey!"

Joey looked around before answering. Louie was holding tight to a sobbing Dexter, Jessica had tear tracks on her face, and Misty was looking at his eyes. He took Misty into his arms. When he looked at Nicholas, his face was defeated...and, strangely, at peace. "It's okay, Nicky. We're done. Game over. She was our ticket out."

Everyone heard his words, and Misty began crying. Realization sank in.

They were trapped in Hell.

Demons began creeping toward them, perhaps realizing that there was no hurry to capture the intruders.

A sudden burst of white light disintegrated the nearest demons, as the light appeared within the group.

"TO ME! NOW!"

It was Cindi Moore. Cindi was an angel.

Chapter 13

An impenetrable dome of white power had been reestablished around the group.

"Cindi?" said Nicholas questioningly.

Joey stared incredulously at the new angel. Power cascaded strongly from Cindi's shoulders, and it seemed much more powerful than Madeline's cascades had been. The angel's visage was brighter and far more powerful than anything he had seen coming from Madeline. Cindi glowed far brighter and far stronger than Madeline, and her eyes had a deeper blue glow.

"GATHER AROUND ME NOW! EACH OF YOU HOLD HANDS AS BEST YOU CAN, OR TOUCH EACH OTHER WHEN YOU CAN'T. WE MUST LEAVE THIS PLACE NOW!"

"But...Cindi...Madeline isn't breathing!" said Nicholas. He had tears running from his eyes.

"I CANNOT HELP MADELINE IN THIS PLACE! ONCE WE RETURN TO YOUR REALM, I WILL SEE WHAT I CAN DO FOR HER."

"And what about Megan? Do we just abandon her?" asked Dexter.

"WE CAN DO NOTHING FOR MEGAN. I'M SORRY."

"But she's my *wife!*" Dexter again tried to break free from Louie's strong arms. He couldn't escape.

"I'M SORRY, DEXTER BECK. WE CAN'T HELP HER NOW. WE MUST LEAVE."

The group gathered around Nicholas's part-time secretary. Jessica and Misty held Cindi's hands, and made certain that everyone was touching in some fashion.

"We're ready," said Jessica.

And, with a thought from the angel, the group winked out of Hell.

MARCUS SMILED AT KAREN. "You're right, punkinhead. I have to have faith in Madeline. I've seen some of the stuff she's done, and..."

A strong breeze began circulation through the situation room. Papers flew around the room. Meredith and Karen both squinted their eyes as their hair blew around their faces.

The group abruptly appeared in the center of the room. Each person collapsed onto the floor. Tony, seeing Cindi, drew his weapon from its holster, but he held it at his side.

"Tony! Get Doc Bishop here! *NOW!*" shouted Joey.

Tony drew his radio and began to speak into it.

Meredith, Karen, Turk, and Marcus noticed that Madeline was lying in the arms of her father. She was so very still. She also had changed back to the form of a little girl. No hint of an angel remained.

"Jessica! CPR! Now!" said Joey urgently. "Misty! Please help her." He turned to Dexter and Louie. "Dexter, I need Louie. Will you be all right for a few minutes?"

Dexter didn't respond at first. Then, he nodded.

Louie relaxed his grip on his friend. Dexter settled slowly to a sitting position, and began crying quietly.

Jessica and Misty had gently taken Madeline from Nicholas, and laid her on the floor. They began CPR calmly and efficiently, even though they were panicking inside over the loss of Megan and the little girl.

Nicholas crouched anxiously beside them. Meredith and Karen rushed to his side, and Karen began talking quietly to Madeline.

"Come on, winghead, you need to come back! We love you, Madeline, and Daddy needs you so badly!"

Joey and Louie went to Marcus, who looked over the group. He then looked into Joey's eyes.

"Megan?"

"She didn't make it, Marcus."

Marcus had nothing to say.

"We know where the children are hidden."

It took a moment for Joey's words to register with Marcus. He looked up at Joey, wide-eyed. "What?"

"We found McGee. We know where the children are hidden. Louie and I can go get them. We just have time."

"No. I'll send bomb squad agents. They're loaded and ready. You two stay here. You're needed." Marcus took his phone from his pocket. "Tell me where," he said, as he spoke into his phone.

"They're in an old, beat-up barge tied to a dock down at the bay. It's not at the main bay docks, though. It's at..." Joey rattled off the address.

"And the booby traps?"

"They're real, all right. I can tell the bomb squad how to dismantle them once they're in place."

Marcus began speaking urgently into his phone.

Doctor Orval Eugene (call me "Buddy") Bishop rushed into the situation room. Two physician's assistants followed, with a bed, IV units, and equipment.

"Where's the..." Bishop began, then he saw Madeline, and the CPR being performed on her. He immediately began rattling off what he needed. "Paddles! Now! We gotta shock her!"

"*WAIT!*"

Cindi, largely forgotten by everyone, had gone to Madeline.

"Let me in. I can help her," Cindi said to Jessica and Misty.

The ladies moved.

Nicholas and his family watched as Cindi knelt beside Madeline. Cindi began changing as she knelt, however, and the visage of a middle-aged woman slowly melted away, leaving a small boy of around ten years old in her place. The boy put his hands on either side of Madeline's head, and closed his eyes. White power began flowing from his hands into Madeline's temples. Her head began to glow with white power, and spread down throughout her body. She took a sudden breath, and began breathing normally. The boy opened his eyes, looked at Madeline, and nodded. He stood and faced Nicholas.

"She is alive."

Meredith and Karen burst into tears and held each other. Nicholas began smiling broadly.

"Thank you. Thank you, Cindi...but, your name isn't really Cindi, is it?"

The boy smiled and shook his head. "No. You may call me Michael." He turned to look down at Madeline. "I came to try to prevent this all from happening, but my father's plans are often unstoppable, even when there is freedom of choice." He turned to look at Nicholas again. "Madeline is, and always has been, my friend. I wanted to help her, if it was possible. And if it was allowed." He smiled. "It seems as if it was both possible *and* allowed." His smile broadened. "I have also helped keep Madeline's word. Gary McGee is in Limbo, as promised."

Nicholas looked at the boy. "Michael? As in...?"

The boy smiled. "I must take your leave now, Nicholas Turner. I don't know if she will remember that she is an angel, but the power is inside her, and she lives. Nothing has been taken from her. Her memory of what she is may yet return. Treasure your daughter, and treasure her love."

The young boy faded from sight.

"D-Daddy?"

Nicholas looked at Madeline. Her eyes were open, and she was looking at the people surrounding her.

"Hi, sweetpea!" said Nicholas.

"Daddy, why am I in the floor? What happened?" Madeline began to try to sit up.

Meredith and Karen were there in an instant.

"Madeline Louise, you will stay where you are until Doctor Bishop says it is okay for you to get up!" Meredith was stern.

"Yeah, winghead, stay put 'till the Doc says you can get up."

Doctor Bishop chose that moment to step forward. "All righty, little lady, let's check you out. Gotta make sure the machine is running properly." He took out his stethoscope, and began his examination.

Joey was on the phone with the bomb squad. The agents had arrived at the barge. Joey explained in detail what had to be done to disarm the booby traps. "Once you've done that, the hatch can be safely opened."

Silence in the room as everyone waited for the bomb squad to respond.

Joey smiled, and said to everyone, "They're in, and the children are all safe."

Everyone began cheering and giving high fives.

Doctor Bishop smiled at Madeline, and said, "Well, looks like you did it, kid."

Madeline looked puzzled. "But what did I do? I don't remember!"

No one else heard her question.

Doctor Bishop continued his examination.

MARCUS TOOK CHARGE of the press conference. He made certain that Justice Security was given all credit for finding the kidnapped children's location.

"I can't go into details about the operation. The details have been designated "Top Secret", and can't be disclosed. I can tell you, however, that the operation was carried out by Justice Security. The information was obtained at great loss to them, and proved to be accurate. We owe another huge debt of gratitude to Joey Justice and Justice Security. No questions."

NICHOLAS AND MEREDITH sat in Doctor Bishop's office.

The doctor had taken Madeline to his examination rooms in Medical, on the first floor. He had asked her parents to wait in the waiting area until he was finished. Jessica had taken Karen to the cafeteria for ice cream.

"What's the prognosis, Doctor?" asked Nicholas.

Doctor Bishop smiled, and said, "We're waiting for one more person, Nicholas."

Three raps sounded from the door, and it eased open. Joey Justice peered in. "Ready for me, Doc?"

"Come in, Joey."

Joey entered the office, closed the door, and leaned against it.

"Okay, let's begin," said Doctor Bishop. "Madeline is in perfect physical health for a little girl her age."

"If that is true, Doctor, then why are we here?" asked Meredith.

Doctor Bishop leaned back in his chair. "She's in perfect *physical* health. However, mentally, she has lost most of her memories of being an angel."

KAREN SLIPPED AWAY from Jessica easily.

The little girl was determined to find her sister. Some things were better left between sisters, and Karen wanted to make sure that Madeline was really okay.

Karen walked into Medical. She peeked into each door's window until she saw Madeline sitting on the edge of a bed swinging her legs. Karen opened the door.

"Hey, winghead!"

Madeline looked puzzled. "Why are you calling me that, Karen?"

Karen looked at Madeline with a weird look. "Because you're an angel, Madeline."

"An angel?"

"Well, duh! Yeah!"

Madeline looked frightened. "I...I don't know what that means!" She began to cry.

Karen hugged Madeline. "Hey, it's okay, Maddie! You can't help it if you can't remember! Don't cry!"

Madeline sobbed while Karen hugged her.

"SO, HER MEMORIES MAY come back. I can find no physical reason that would prevent it. But, she may become frustrated and upset about the memory loss."

"But she's okay otherwise?" asked Nicholas.

Doctor Bishop smiled and nodded. "As I said, she's a perfectly healthy little girl."

Meredith said, "You have said that twice, Doctor. Do you have a point?"

Realization hit Nicholas, and his eyes widened. "I get it! She's a *little girl*, Meredith! She doesn't remember how to be an angel! She's *real*, and she's in the *real world!*"

"And Nicholas gets the cigar," said Doctor Bishop.

"I still do not understand," said Meredith.

"Honey, if Madeline is going to be a regular little girl, with skin and hair and everything that goes with it, *where did she come from?* Where's her paperwork? Where's she been all this time? What's her Social Security number? We can't account for these things!"

Joey said, "Maybe not. But, with help from Marcus, I can." He stood straight. "I bet that by the time we hit Sardis County, we'll have a legitimate birth certificate, immunization records..." He looked meaningfully at Doctor Bishop.

"And I'll see that she has all of her shots," said Bishop.

"And she'll have a real Social Security number, in her name. We'll get it all covered, and you'll have it as soon as we can get it done."

Nicholas looked at Joey. "Thank you, Joey."

Joey shrugged. "Hey, it's what partners do for each other. We'll teach you all of it before you go."

DEXTER SAT QUIETLY in the evening darkness. His thoughts wandered all over the place.

I can't believe she's really gone. No more laughter, no more calming her down when she's angry...that time she jumped out of the plywood cake that Joey and Marcus made for my birthday and did a striptease. That was a really fun night. Hector met her for the first time that night, and he was so proud of his sister-in-law. What am I going to do without her?

Someone knocked on the front door of his sixth floor apartment.

Dexter ignored it.

Someone knocked again.

"Go *away*, Louie!"

A timid, small voice said quietly, "I'm not Louie."

Dexter realized who the voice belonged to. He rose, walked to the front door, and opened it.

"Hello, Madeline."

The little girl stood, head down, with her hands knotted together in front of her. She was sneaking peeks at Dexter through her brown bangs.

"Hello."

Both were silent for a few seconds. Madeline spoke first.

"Karen said that she heard that you lost Megan trying to protect me."

"Yes."

Madeline cocked one foot behind her. "I'm sorry."

Dexter looked at Madeline. This time, he noticed that she had tear tracks on either side of her face. He could hear Megan inside his head. *Baby, she thinks it's her fault. You have to make sure that she knows that I chose to protect her, and that I knew what I was getting into.*

"Madeline."

"Yes, sir?" Madeline wouldn't look at him.

Dexter said, "Look at me, honey."

The little girl raised her head, and met Dexter's eyes.

"It isn't your fault, Madeline." Dexter held his arms open. "Come here."

Madeline sobbed, and rushed into Dexter's arms. They hugged tightly, and both sobbed quietly over what they'd been through.

Neither one noticed Jessica at the corner of the hall. She had come to talk to Dexter, and to help him with his grief, but saw that Madeline had gotten there first. She wisely kept her presence to herself as Dexter and Madeline mourned to themselves.

Chapter 14

The Justice Security lobby was packed.

All of the chairs in front of the raised dais were filled, with the exception of the ones reserved for partners and their families, and dozens more people lined the walls and empty spaces around it. Today's memorial service would be broadcast across the company radios. Microphones were connected and in place.

Marcus Moore had already taken his seat. Joey had told him earlier that nobody know whether Dexter would actually show up for Megan's service.

"He won't talk about it with anyone, Marcus," Joey had said. "I'm afraid that he's blaming Louie for keeping him from going after Megan."

Marcus had replied, "From what you told me, doesn't Dexter realize that Louie didn't want to risk losing both of them?"

"I think, deep down, he knows that. But he hasn't spoken to Louie since then. Not a word."

That had been yesterday.

Marcus prayed fervently that Dexter would come to the memorial today.

Mark Haase was at the reception desk. At ten-fifty-five, he had instructions to lock the lobby doors. The memorial service was a private affair...no general public.

Miriam Apple and Steve, her cameraman, walked into the lobby at ten-fifty-four. Mark didn't stop them. They had no equipment, and were there at Joey's personal invitation.

Mark locked the doors.

At eleven o'clock, the partners and families of Justice Security walked slowly from the elevators to their seats.

As they sat, an empty chair was left in place. On one side, Percival "King Louie" Washington sat. On the other side sat Madeline. The empty seat was for Dexter.

At eleven-oh-five, Joey stood. He then climbed the three steps to the raised dais, and took the place behind the podium. The room was silent, and Joey scanned the room.

Still no Dexter. Damn.

Joey took a breath, and began to speak.

"Those of us at Justice Security, from the partners down to the janitorial staff, work hard at our jobs. It doesn't matter whether we're working for our clients, or for our fellow staff members. We work hard."

Joey stopped. A slight murmur had come from the crowd beside the elevators. The doors slid open. Dexter stood there.

In unison, every single employee of Justice Security that was present in the lobby ran a thumb over a lighter, and they silently held high a flame.

Dexter proudly walked to his seat. One tear ran down his cheek. He sat down silently.

Louie reached out and patted Dexter on the back. Madeline took his hand.

Joey continued.

"One of the hardest parts of *my* work is happening right now. A memorial service is never easy to do, but I always do it willingly, and without a second thought. To me, it's a way to honor those members of Justice Security that have given their all for us."

He drank from the water bottle that was on the podium.

"Some memorial services are harder than others." Joey looked down at the podium, then raised his eyes. "What do you do when it's someone that's as close to you as Megan was to all of us? Really, what do you say? What *can* you say?" He gestured to Dexter. "How do we tell this man how much his wife meant to all of us?" Joey shook his head.

"Megan Fisk Beck earned her stripes as a Justice Security partner. She has figured out tremendous data processing problems. She has been wounded in the field. She has earned our trust, our respect, and our love. She was never so busy that she didn't take time out to give weapon pointers and advice to anyone that needed it. Megan was our friend and confidante."

Joey scanned the audience from left to right.

"I can't share the details of how we lost her. That part's classified by the FBI." He paused. "Are we going to miss her? Oh, yeah. Am *I* going to miss her? You bet your ass I am." He paused again. "But it's nothing compared to what

Dexter is feeling. We lost our friend, our co-worker, our partner. Dexter *lost his wife*." Joey looked down at Dexter. "My friend, I don't know what I'd do without Misty. Anything you need, from any of us, any time at all...please just ask. We'll all take care of you."

Madeline began clapping. Louie followed. Soon, the entire lobby was applauding, not from joy, but from solidarity...and support.

Realizing that there was nothing else to say, Joey took the plaque that held Megan's name, and hung it in its place on the honor wall.

LATER, IN JOEY'S OFFICE, Joey, Misty, Nicholas, and Meredith were gathered around the big coffee table. Each had a small drink.

"I believe that this has been the saddest I have been since my first husband passed away," observed Meredith.

"I'll drink to that," replied Joey. He was on his fourth drink.

"I can't help but feel it's my fault that she's gone," said Nicholas.

"Please don't spread that nonsense, Nicky," said Misty. "We were there. It could have been any of us. It just happened to be Megan."

"But it was my daughter that you all were protecting."

"If it's *anybody's* fault, it's mine," said Joey. "I'm the one that suggested that Madeline take us to Hell, for God's sake. If I'd just kept my mouth shut, Megan would still be here, and Madeline would still be an angel."

Misty quietly said, "And those children and their bus driver would be dead, Joey."

Joey drained his glass. "Yeah. But was it worth the cost?"

Misty slapped at Joey's arm. "Joey Justice! How can you say such a thing?"

Joey shrugged.

Meredith said, "I noticed that Madeline was holding Dexter's hand during the memorial service. Although, it appeared that Dexter was holding Madeline's hand instead. I believe that he would not agree with you, Joey."

Joey grunted, and rose to fix himself another drink. "This business is getting harder on me, I guess. We've had more deaths since we met Fernandez than I would have believed possible."

"And yours was almost one of them in Chicago," replied Misty.

"Joey, here's a little piece of wisdom that I've picked up over the years: Don't be afraid to put it all on the line for what you believe is right. Be ready to die for it, if need be. I was ready, and so was Madeline."

"What will you do if Madeline never remembers her life as an angel?" asked Misty.

"I'll take Michael's advice, and cherish every moment with my daughter."

Meredith patted Nicholas on the arm. "*Our* daughter, dear."

Nicholas smiled at his wife. "Of course, honey."

"Okay, enough of this. Work awaits." Joey tossed his drink back, and put the glass down on the bar. "Nicholas, Marcus said that we'll have all of our paperwork on Madeline by next week. Judge Stone has signed the adoption papers on Karen for you, and she's signed adoption papers on Madeline for Meredith. Doc Bishop has given Madeline all immunizations that are required for a child her age, and will follow up on them as he visits you at the second location. We've set up some things that indicate that she has been away at boarding school."

Nicholas chuckled. "What's the name of the school?"

Joey smiled. "Justice Academy. The phone number rings into Turk's phone. It's a dedicated line, in case any of the schools in Sardis County have questions. As smart as Madeline is, she's enrolled as a high school freshman with our 'academy.'"

"Do you truly think she is ready for that level, Joey?" asked Meredith.

Joey nodded. "I do. She has knowledge that hasn't been tapped yet. I can see her graduating from high school within a couple of years...unless the school system in Sardis County is completely backward, and reluctant to promote by merit."

"Have you two decided what you'll do for housing?" asked Misty.

Meredith smiled. "We have."

Nicholas laughed. "We plan to live in the new building for a while. We're keeping the house here. We'll just close it up and hold on to it. For now, anyway. If we like Sardis County, we may sell the house later, and buy something there."

Joey nodded. "Good plan." He sat down on the love seat beside Misty. "Nicky, I'm heading there next week. Want to come? If it's okay with Meredith, of course." He leaned back. "I thought I'd go check on everything, and introduce myself to the sheriff there. It wouldn't be more than a couple of days."

Nicholas and Meredith shared a look. It was one of the looks that two people that are very close to each other have that can communicate an entire conversation without speaking a word.

Nicholas said, "I'll go with you. I'd like to check out progress on the building myself." He smiled. "Snickers may be ready to go with us, if you're willing. When he gave his notice to the place that he worked, they said it could be effective immediately. So, he's tying up loose ends around here. Says he's going to miss McFeely's Bar, though."

Joey smiled. "Yeah, we know Hank very well. Tell Snickers he can go with us. He can even stay, if he wants to."

Chapter 15

The Justice Security building had a small park-like area outside. It contained a couple of shade trees, lots of benches, and a picnic table. It was open to anyone, which meant that the public could use it, as well as Justice Security personnel.

Madeline and Karen sat side-by-side on one of the benches. They were the only people in the park.

"Winghead, do you remember anything about being an angel?" asked Karen.

Madeline's brow furrowed. "I can remember talking to Daddy with only our minds. I remember rescuing you from those bad guys, but I don't remember how I did it. I can remember fading your stuff, but I don't remember how I did that, either." She stared off into the distance. "And I know that I prayed a lot." Madeline smiled. "I guess I can still do that. One thing that I don't have to remember."

"Do you think you'll ever remember it all?"

Madeline thought about it. "I hope so, Karen. I really do. I remember helping Daddy, and helping to keep all of you safe...and *I can't do it now!* That's what bothers me the most about it!"

Karen thought for a moment. "Madeline, we're kids. Both of us. Maybe we aren't 'sposed to do anything *except* be kids."

Madeline was quiet, and so was Karen. They watched the traffic on the street, and the people walking along the sidewalks.

"So what do you think about moving to Sardis County? To Perry?" asked Karen.

"I think it's what we should do," answered Madeline. "It feels right somehow."

"And look at you! The high school freshman!"

Madeline smirked. "I think Joey doesn't' know what he's talking about. But that's okay. He means well." She crossed her hands across her stomach. "I think this move will be good for us. I feel like we're going to be part of something big." She shrugged. "It's just a feeling, though."

They sat quietly.

Karen said, "Wanna go play in the gym? Louie said we could."

Madeline jumped up. "Sure! Race you!"

The girls got to the gym at the same time. Louie was there, and both girls jumped on him as they giggled.

About The Author: T. M. Bilderback is a former radio announcer with a number of story ideas running around inside his head, most based on or inspired by classic songs. The author currently resides in Tennessee, and is writing feverishly in order to banish these stories from his head and into book form before he runs screaming into the street.

Other works by T. M. Bilderback

Nicholas Turner
  If You Could Read My Mind
Justice Security
Mama Told Me Not To Come
Someone Saved My Life Tonight
Jackie Blue
Wake Me Up Before You Go-Go
Saturday In The Park
MacArthur Park
The Little Drummer Boy
The Night Chicago Died
Jim Dandy
Cow Patty
Hell's Bells
Tales Of Sardis County
Don't Come Around Here No More
Junior's Farm
The Devil's In The Details
I'm Your Boogie Man
Colonel Abernathy's Tales
The Lion Sleeps Tonight
Heart Of Glass
Other Stories
The Wreck Of The Edmund Fitzgerald
Gold
Hot Child In The City
Eli's Coming
Other Novels
Empty Eyes
Short Story Collections
Greatest Hits

Don't miss out!

Visit the website below and you can sign up to receive emails whenever T. M. Bilderback publishes a new book. There's no charge and no obligation.

https://books2read.com/r/B-A-KAW-KMIY

BOOKS 2 READ

Connecting independent readers to independent writers.

Also by T. M. Bilderback

Colonel Abernathy's Tales

The Lion Sleeps Tonight - A Short Story

Le Lion Est Mort Ce Soir - Une Nouvelle

El León Duerme Esta Noche - Un Cuento

Leul Doarme În Noaptea Aceasta - O Povestire

Quem Dorme É O Leão - Um Conto

Il Leone Dorme Stanotte - Un Racconto Breve

Heart Of Glass - A Short Story

Justice Security

Mama Told Me Not To Come - A Justice Security Novel

Someone Saved My Life Tonight - A Justice Security Short Story

Alguém Salvou Minha Vida Esta Noite - Um Conto da Cia. Justo de Segurança

Anoche, Alguien Me Salvó La Vida - Un Cuento Sobre Un Guardia De Justice Security

Stanotte Qualcuno Mi Ha Salvato La Vita - Un Racconto Da Justice Security

Jackie Blue - A Justice Security Novel

Wake Me Up Before You Go-Go - A Justice Security Novel

Saturday In The Park - A Justice Security Short Story

Sábado En El Parque - Un Cuento Sobre Un Guardia de Justice Security

Sabato Al Parco – Un Racconto Della Justice Security

Sábado no Parque - Um Conto da Cia. Justo de Segurança

MacArthur Park - A Justice Security Short Story

Parque MacArthur – Un Cuento Sobre Un Guardia de Justice Security
MacArthur Park – Un Racconto Della Justice Security
Parque MacArthur - Um Conto da Cia. Justo de Segurança
The Little Drummer Boy - A Justice Security Short Story
Il Piccolo Tamburino - Un Racconto Della Justice Security
El Pequeño Tamborilero - Un Relato De Justice Security
O Pequeno Baterista - Um Conto Da CIA. Justo De Segurança
The Night Chicago Died - A Justice Security Novel
Jim Dandy - A Justice Security Novel
Cow Patty - A Justice Security Novel
Hell's Bells - A Justice Security Novel
Black Dog - A Justice Security Novel
Lido Shuffle - A Justice Security Novel

Tales Of Sardis County
Don't Come Around Here No More - A Tale Of Sardis County
Non Fatevi Vedere Mai Piu' - Un Racconto Della Contea Di Sardis
Não Apareçam Mais Aqui - Uma História do Município de Sardis
No Vuelvas Nunca Más – Una Historia Del Condado De Sardis
Junior's Farm - A Tale Of Sardis County
A Fazenda Do Junior - Um Conto Sobre O Condado de Sardis
The Devil's In The Details - A Tale Of Sardis County
I'm Your Boogie Man - A Tale Of Sardis County

Standalone
Greatest Hits
If You Could Read My Mind - A Nicholas Turner Novel
The Wreck Of The Edmund Fitzgerald - A Short Story
Eli's Coming - A Short Story
Empty Eyes
Gold - A Short Story
Hot Child In The City - A Short Story